To Jeane

Valorous

An Affliction of Falling Novel
By: Kristina Canady

Love always
wins

xoxo

Cataloging-in-Publication Date is on-file at the Library of Congress

Book design/formatting by Kristina Canady
Cover design and layout by Sassy Queens of Design
Cover Model Drew Truckle
Photo of Drew Truckle by Eric Battershell Photography
Photograph of Golden Gate Bridge and Lanterns purchased Stock photo
Editing Acknowledgments: Cynthia Shepp

Note from the author:

In lieu of a traditional blurb or dedication, I thought I would write from the heart. You see, Jade's story is personal for me—a raw, collective idea that crawled from the depths of pain I vicariously experienced by way of caring for a patient population very dear to my heart. This story has taken me a few years to tell. Many times, the pure emotions evoked from these characters as they evolved became too overwhelming, prompting a need for a break.

I actually started writing this story before Scrupulous, but I battled with wanting to tell it just right. I didn't want to let down those who can personally relate to the trials and tribulations these characters endure. Cancer doesn't care. It is a dark, insatiable illness, consuming all that it can in its path. Cancer can make or break not only a person, but also the family and friends championing alongside the warrior battling to heal their body and reclaim their life.

My love and respect for oncology patients and their support systems of amazing people is never ending. My hope is that you connect with this next installment of the Affliction of Falling Series, that I do this story a fraction of the justice it deserves, and entice you to continue to explore the multifaceted struggles of falling in love during difficult and non-conventional circumstances.

Please enjoy this tale of love, loss, and the joys of rediscovering one's own strength and ability love again.

Chapter 1

<u>Jade</u>

The rain pounds sideways against my coat, seeping deviously down through the tops of my rubber boots, clinging to every bit of exposed flesh or cloth it can find around my gear. Quite the metaphor for the night we had last night. Ducking in to my sanctuary for shelter from the torrential downpour, I quickly shake off my umbrella with a rattle and place it by the door alongside a few others. Pausing for a moment, I let my eyes drift over the lined-up, collapsed soldiers, rivulets of water dripping off their folded-in arms. My emotions attempt to get the better of me as my mind drifts into associations I'd rather not dwell on.

When I inhale deeply, aromas of roasted java waft over my senses, quelling my stress like a salve on impact. The subtle sounds of intimate conversations among the surrounding patrons mingles with the grinding of espresso beans and steaming of milk, perfectly drowning out the incessant, tumultuous thoughts nagging me. A sense of peace falls over my shaking body as I slowly warm while waiting in line to get my usual. The person in front of me moves to the side, allowing me to approach the cashier. My order slowly tumbles from my lips before my numb body floats in a haze to the end of the counter to wait for it. I focus on the fluctuating, surrounding tempos that accompany a busy coffee joint on a rainy,

San Francisco morning, and the rapid beating of my heart begins to slow.

Someone calls my name and sets my order out to my left, startling me partially out of my autopilot. Reminding myself to breathe, I collect my little cup of heaven, and then stalk off to my favorite bistro table by the big window, not far off from the fireplace. Pulling back my damp, dirty blond hair, I lasso it into an overstretched tie from my wrist. When finished, I quickly take out my charcoal pencils and sketchpad from my leather messenger bag. It takes me a moment to arrange everything in front of me before any serious work can begin. As I take another deep, cleansing breath, my hand finds my cup, and I relish a sip from my liquid gold. The dark beverage slowly slides down my throat as I savor the taste flowing across my taste buds. I now feel centered. My free hand subconsciously picks up my graphite pencil and begins sketching away.

It is in this transcended state that bliss is found, slipped into a portal where linear time does not exist. Unconscious downloads from beyond filter into me and out through my working hand. Images begin to fill the page, forming something I initially had no direct intentions of creating. Sure, I might have an inclining thought of what I want to create when I start, but in the end, something else, something bigger than imagined, takes over as the art manifests into this world, my hands simply a tool while I connect to that place beyond. A place where pain doesn't exist in the same concept as it does here.

After a while, my hand begins to cramp, and I withdraw from that meditative state, seeking caffeine-driven fuel. It's not long before I begin to feel like I am being watched. Self-consciously, I look up in the direction I feel it coming from to find a devastatingly handsome man seated in the wingback by the fire. He has his gaze zeroed in on me. His coppery red hair glints in the low light as his sparkling blue eyes focus in on my mismatched ones. My breath catches in my chest as the instant connection stifles my diaphragm's ability to expand and contract.

Holy cow, what is this? My nostrils flair and my eyes go wide as heat floods me, brain kicking back in from the short-lived, state of stupid it just slipped into. Surely, he is not looking at me. My cheeks burn as my gaze casts back down to my sketchpad, and I dismiss the uneasy feeling as coincidence. Quickly clearing my mind and shaking the odd feelings away, I force my hands to get back to work. Today is a big day. We will finally get the results from Jack's tests. With an hour to spare before I am expected back across the street at the hospital, I allow my art to consume me, to wash away my fear and pain so that I can be strong for my husband. This has become my daily routine, escaping to my safe haven first thing in the morning to grasp some normalcy—away from the antiseptic smells and constant beeping and humming of machines. An hour to myself to regroup and put my brave face back on. He deserves nothing less.

∞

"Hey, sexy! How's my gorgeous wife this morning?" Jack beams as I try to quietly enter his room. My heart rate speeds right back up into overdrive as my hand instinctively clutches my chest.

"I thought you were still sleeping. I was trying not to wake you." I sigh, shake the start he gave me off, and scamper up to his bed. I'm afraid to get too close, as he is looking worse than usual, so I kiss him lightly on the lips. Intuitively, my mind tells me exactly what news we are going to get today.

"Hmmm, you taste delicious. I wish I could savor that coffee on your lips." He grins, attempting to flirt with me, but his hallowed eyes and raspy voice from coughing all night speak louder, pummeling my eardrums with the truth.

"Or I could get you a coffee," I urge, slipping on my mask of control and caretaking as I sit on the edge of his bed and lean into him.

"Wish I could drink it. You know everything tastes like ass these days." He grimaces at the thought of trying to eat. Even in this sickly state, he is still handsome—my husband for whom the sun will always rise and set around.

Brushing back his soft brown hair, I stare into his chocolate-brown eyes, wishing I could fix everything for him, or at least take away the bulk of his debilitating symptoms. I am his wife; I should be able to do that for the love of my life. Sorrow beats at me as I berate myself. Most days, I feel helpless as I watch him hold steadfast in his personal war with cancer with the unwavering commitment and dedication of a warrior. Jack is my hero, and I can only hope to be even half as strong as he.

"You have to try to eat something," I nag.

"Okay, Mom," he teases as he leans in to rest his head on my shoulder, inhaling deeply to breathe me in.

A light knock sounds before the nurse walks in, shoulders down, lines of worry set deep in her mature face, with a white coat hot on her heels. She's one of the few nurses who have gone out of her way to make sure she cares for Jack every time she is here. She's also one of the few who have been able to help me coerce him into creature comforts like dessert, showers, and fresh linen on the bed. Jack is used to being the caretaker, finding joy in always doing for others whether they asked or not. He's absolutely despised needing others to do for him. She even went out of her way to make him is favorite dessert, a buttery pecan pie. He ate an entire piece before politely giving the rest to the staff, which was more than he'd eaten in days. I normally despise pecan pie, but hers was a slice of heaven.

"Good morning, Mr. and Mrs. Ritter. I am Dr. Brown, filling in for Dr. Monroe today. I've come to review your test results with you, and see where you would like to go from here," Dr. Brown casually informs us, his face impassive. For whatever reason, I already don't like him. Jack nods, and I take his hand as my heart lurches into my throat like a ball of destruction, ready to rip me apart. "Very good. As you know, you have non-Hodgkin's lymphoma and have finished three full rounds of chemotherapy. After having to admit you to the hospital once again for further testing due to your extremely high fevers in the presence of your neutropenia and abnormal blood tests, Dr. Monroe felt it necessary to repeat your PET scan now instead of after your next round of chemotherapy.

"Now, I know that you had one done after your second round, but this PET scan shows that your lymphoma is much more aggressive than we thought, and it has spread further. Considering your scan, biopsy, and blood work results, I think it is safe to assume you have rapidly progressed to stage four."

Dr. Monroe's voice begins to fade to the background as I become lost in the meaning of what he is saying. We knew treatment was going to be a bumpy road. When Jack was diagnosed, he was already at stage three before we figured out what was wrong with him. He is young… *we* are young. The fact he has developed this horrific disease at the age of twenty-nine is baffling. We had just bought our first house and were trying for a baby when he fell ill, which prompted the forward-moving freight train that is now barreling down on us now. We thought we'd nip this damn thing fast and get on with starting a family.

Dr. Monroe is one of the top oncology doctors in San Francisco. He had been confident that given Jack's age and otherwise healthy state, he had a hell of a fighting chance. Shit, all the research I'd done said he'd have about a 57-68 percent chance of survival. Sure, the odds were not *that* great, but they were a whole hell of a lot better than some of the other cancers I obsessively researched out of morbid curiosity.

"Babe?" Jack asks, bringing my attention back around to the present situation.

"Yes?"

"What do you think?" His clammy hand squeezes mine.

"About?" Shame floods me. I should have been paying attention instead of panicking.

"Treatment options. What do you think I should do? Stick with the chemo, do chemo and radiation, or throw in the towel?" he asks with all seriousness, but he throws on the last bit with a hint of sarcasm. Jack will never give up; he is one of the most persistent people I have ever met, aside from my best friend.

"We give it everything we've got." In truth, I don't know what I want, but I know it is he wants to hear. What else do you tell the love of your life under these circumstances?

"Well, Doc, you heard the little woman. Balls to the wall it is," Jack smarts as the doctor clenches his jaw, unfamiliar with Jack's charm.

The doctor recovers. "Very well. Being that your blood work and x-ray have come back with no signs of infection to attribute to your fevers, we will have to sum them up as neutropenic fevers and push on with treatment. We will begin tomorrow." Dr. Brown communicates a few more things to the nurse before promptly leaving.

It has been just a few months since he was originally diagnosed. He fell ill at the end of summer, but he wasn't diagnosed properly for weeks after. He started his first round at beginning of October. Now, here we are, end of January, a few weeks past our one-year anniversary. Jack had a wicked sense of humor. We got married on New Year's at his insistence. He didn't want me to ever forget our anniversary. He also loved the idea that everyone would be celebrating around the world at the same time. Normally, the wife is the one fretting about her husband remembering such things. Jack knew me well. I can barely remember what day of the week it is, and I would be lost without my day planner. Yes, most use their cell phones, but I prefer paper and pen to electronics any day.

"You okay?" Jack asks me as he strokes my arm. He is always trying to comfort me and think of my needs, even though he is the one who is sick. The consideration makes me wonder if his persistence through all of this really has to do with the fact that he feels like he has to hang on for me?

"Don't you worry about me, silly. Keep those brain cells focused on kicking that evil demon's ass that is trying to possess my husband. I have plans for you, mister. I refuse to give you up. We have too many things to do. You are not getting out of all my travel plans for us that easily."

"Damn. I mean, of course, dear." He laughs. Jack and I love to travel. He'd planned to take me to Europe this summer to tour the countless museums. As I am an art and art history teacher, I am a geek for all things museum. He doesn't care much for them, but did it to humor me. Jack would rather experience the different cultures… food primarily. But, that all seems lost to the wind now.

After talking to the doctor in the hall, the nurse comes back in to begin her monitoring. I manage to sluggishly get up, even with the thousand-pound weight on my shoulders, and move over to the chair by the window so that I am not in the way. Gazing at my warm and loving husband, I send up a silent prayer as the nurse examines him. He has become so thin lately. For a man who lives for all things food, he can barely stand to eat now. The chemo eradicated his taste buds. I won't give up, I will find something he can stomach and enjoy if it's the last thing I do.

My phone beeps with an incoming text, and I quickly reply before putting the phone away. Sorcha and Gavin wanted to come by and bring us dinner. I have been deflecting everyone, but those two might just be a welcome distraction. Knowing them, they'll traipse down to the older part of China Town and bring some tasty delights from that back-alley place that can cook any five-star restaurant under the bridge.

Chapter 2

<u>Jade</u>

Slipping out from the foldout couch's covers in the wee hours of the morning, I quickly ready, trying to be as quiet as possible. My darling husband shifts, as if he may be trying to rise, when I slip my socks on, but the weight of exhaustion wins, pulling him back under. His restless body settles. Grabbing my boots and belongings, I quickly pad out the door. It isn't until my body is outside of his room, the door gently latched behind me, that I take a deep breath. Sliding the messenger bag strap over my shoulder, I nod to our night nurse, who's rapidly trying to chart so she can get home, and head out to seek respite at the posh little coffee shop across the street.

After ordering my usual in a typical morning daze, I plop down at my little table and ceremoniously set up shop in a clumsy clatter of pencils and shuffling of papers. Today, I have a crap ton of essays to grade and a class to teach tonight. My boss offered to get me a sub for the rest of the year, stated that it would be best for me considering the circumstances, but I refused. I plan to take the summer off to care for Jack, so I need to finish up this semester. Perhaps I insisted more for my own sanity. It has become too easy to be absorbed by the senselessness of all that encompasses fighting this horrendous illness that doesn't give two shits about anything or anyone. It takes without asking, it doesn't discriminate, and it is utterly ridiculous. My insides flip and panic grips my breath as I hurriedly tuck the emotions attempting to overwhelm me back under the rug. Taking a deep, cleansing breath, I smell the aromas all around and re-center on the task at hand.

The background noises fade, and time ticks by. I become engrossed in my mountain of papers written by less-than-thrilled students who mutilated facts and patched them together with fiction in the hope I wouldn't notice. The front door opens in the background of the words I am attempting to understand. The brashness of rattled of chimes startles me as a group comes meandering in, laughing quite loudly. Pinpricks of sightless needles suddenly work along the back of my neck as a draft wafts in behind the crowd. My senses heighten as I feel eyes on me once more, an odd feeling in a place of business bustling with patrons. Looking up to search for the offending source, I find the same stranger from a few days ago, staring at me again. My breath catches as waves of foreign sensations crash over me under the weight of his stare. His bright blue eyes are hypnotizing, drawing me in instantly.

The weight behind them chokes my reasonable mind that is screaming, *This is wrong*, but my entire being is overridden. Like a moth to a flame, I am in endanger of succumbing to something I don't even understand. This must be what some speak about, the enigmatic pull of a stranger that can lead to Hollywood movie endings. Certainly, if I believed in that sort of thing, it would be composed from a moment exactly like this. The stranger's piercing blue eyes peruse me from across the room as he waits for the barista to finish his drink.

Perplexed and unable to resist dissecting the phenomena, my eyes trace every line of his body, committing the artistic perfections to memory like a fine sculpture. He is posed against the wall, intently regarding me once more as I shamelessly carry on. His red hair is neatly kept, a bit longer in the front but currently swept back. His masculine jaw and fit build make him look a tad awkward in the suit he is filling out. I imagine he'd fill out a kilt much better, his broad chest bare as he worked the land, his chiseled perfection glistening in the sun.

Where on earth did my mind just go? What the heck is wrong with me? I seriously need to start sleeping instead of staying up all night to keep watch over Jack's every movement. As sick as I feel over where my mind just wandered, I can't escape the fact that this man has stirred something in me I cannot explain. That fact alone doesn't sit well at all.

Drumming my fingers on the wooden bistro table, I heavily scold myself. I try to bring my focus back around to what I am doing instead of the stranger who rapidly inspired some crazy, not to mention highly inappropriate, *Braveheart* fantasies in my head. I seriously must be delusional. Is there such a thing as sympathy chemo brain? Chemo can make you act different, a little crazy even. That would explain the daydream. Yes, that must be exactly what happened. Maybe that shit is in the air on that damn oncology floor, and I am breathing it in. Casting my eyes back down to my mess, my hand searches for my red pen. As my fingers glide over the plastic of my weapon of choice, a figure appears. It throws a large shadow over my table, forcing me to look up at the hovering individual. It is the strange man.

"Good mornin'. Mind if I sit?" he asks with a thick, Scottish accent while motioning to the vacant chair across from me. His deep voice caresses me in a fashion that should never be allowed. Crap! I thought I was just being silly with the kilt thing, now, Lord help me.

"Uh, no, I mean, yes… go ahead," I stammer, trying to figure out what ridiculousness has come over me. He cocks his head. His eyes are clearly amused as he promptly sits down.

"Thank ye, miss. All the seats seem to be takin' at the moment." His eyes glitter as he regards me. "The name is Shae, Shae MacCain." He holds out his large hand in formal reception.

I almost knock my coffee over in a rush to return the greeting, causing myself to fumble like a mess. "Shay? Isn't that a— I knew a girl with the same— I'm sorry! Jade. My name is Jade. Nice to meet you," I stutter, heat flaming to my cheeks.

"No offense taken." He grins in a cool, collected manner, his kind eyes settling on mine.

"I'm sorry; you just caught me off guard." I quickly try to defend my odd behavior, rarely am I the bumbling idiot. In fact, I'm never that at all. My squirrely hands push the stack of papers out of the way to make room, just in time to also knock my pens into a rolling heap that continues onto the floor. "Crap! Sorry." I reach to get them, but he stops me.

"Aye, lass. Allow me?" His assessing gaze is warm; it's as if he can see through me, into my deepest thoughts and fears. Somehow, there is a comfort in his kindness that forces me to retract my reach and allow the help. He sweeps up the runaways and sets them back into the little pouch from which they had escaped. "Sorry to intrude. There's just nowhere else to sit, and I'd rather enjoy this cup before runnin' off to work." He smiles a full-watt stunner, and a little dimple peeks through as he sips his coffee. My heart falters once more before kicking back into a normal pace. I force a deep inhale to ease my body's bizarre reaction. The scent from his cup comes across the table as strong, without the typical creams and flavors most like ruin their beverages with. I respect that.

"It's not a problem. This place tends to get crowded about this time." I nervously tuck the errant waves of my hair behind my ear and blush under the intensity of his regard. See? He hasn't been checking me out. He just wanted a place to sit—a simple explanation.

"What are ye workin' on here? It's a bit early for all this." He motions to the overwhelming stack.

"A peaceful escape from the realities of life." My voice drifts off as sudden emotion attempts to strangle me once more, the timing completely inappropriate. It's confirmed; I am edging my way toward certifiable. Something sparks in his eyes in response as he registers more than he should.

"Aye, well then, that looks quite heavy for escapin', but I can appreciate the sentiments. The red is a bit heavy handed, no?" he jokes as he looks at the current paper I mutilated.

"Well, my students obviously find impressionism quite boring because they aren't even trying to stay on topic." I laugh.

"You're a teacher then?" His interest piques.

"Yeah, art history, and a few painting and drawing classes." Being able to speak about familiar ground begins to settle me in his presence.

"Impressive. I take it ye are a purest, insistin' they write solely on the contributions of impressionism to modern art?" His eyes dance wickedly in an obvious attempt to bait me as he thoughtfully brings his mug to his lips.

"I think it best to stop while you are ahead, Mr. MacCain." I unattractively snort as my confidence fully returns, my feet now on solid ground for the first time in… well, I can't remember when.

"Go on then, educate me." His brow rises.

"It seems you are well educated enough, but if you are asking, the subject matter of the paper was to write about impressionism's focus, the style and drive of the artists who practiced such, and how it gave birth to Neo-impressionism and Postimpressionism. They were also to include the differences in each style. These," I wave my hand at the stack, "lack emotion and true understanding of the movements and how revolutionary they were during their time. It's all regurgitated facts they picked out of Wikipedia."

"Perhaps they just need to be inspired?"

"Perhaps… it's going to be a long semester." I sigh heavily.

"Well, it is in my personal opinion that Postimpressionism was more revolutionary as it allowed the artists' raw emotions to be displayed in a more poetic fashion."

My eyes light up as excitement flutters throughout me. "Yes! Exactly. Are you an art lover, Mr. MacCain?" Goodness me, what a refreshing statement.

"I dabble here and there, more of a modern and abstract man myself."

"Isn't everyone?" I say. "What do you do for a living?"

"I'm an architect. I specialize in restoration of old buildings." He shrugs his shoulders as if it is nothing.

"Really? That sounds fascinating. Are you currently working on any big projects?" My inner art geek has perked up, and it is grasping onto anything non-cancer related.

"Yeah, I've been called into town to help with a few projects." His upper lip quirks as he watches me rudely stare at his mouth. I can't help it; the plump lines are perfect, like Michelangelo's David, but better. Most bodies have a slight asymmetry. It's a natural thing. But not him; it's truly fascinating. I wonder what Michelangelo would say about a specimen like this— he'd probably want to sculpt him immediately.

"Such as…" I encourage him to go on, not wanting the distraction to stop, happy to feel the flare of my artistic side that holds appreciation for creation and the world in general.

"A turn-of-the-century Victorian home up in Pacific Heights as well as a church restoration in that neck of the woods." His thick accent makes me want to question where he is from, yet his career choice pulls at my interests as well; I am conflicted about what to ask next.

"What brings you to this side of town?" *And where are you from, what do you like, and what do you think of our eclectic mix of modern and Victorian architecture here in the city?* This creature has fascinated me. He has enticed me out of my cold, depressive existence.

"I am also consulting across the street on a project for the university."

"In from out of town, and working all over the place it seems."

"I fly across the pond only a few times a year. They know they better book me when I come." His shoulders drop as his large figure leans back.

"Is that right?" My sarcasm is evident in the face of his cocky statement.

"I wasn't aware that UCSF had an art program." He turns the tables.

"They don't. I teach up the street at the University of San Francisco."

"What brings ye down this way then? The coffee is good, but not that good." His tone is careful, thoughtful and, for once, a type of probing that doesn't put me on guard.

"My husband. He's in the hospital across the street." Something about Shae makes me want to let it all out, cry, scream, yell, laugh… release all the pent-up emotions I keep tucked away in order to appear strong for everyone else. Something about his strength and polished yet down-to-earth air commands it.

"I am sorry to hear that. I've seen you all week, every morning, pouring over yer work here at this table. Must be serious?"

"Yeah, he has cancer." There, those simple words I rarely speak, rarely acknowledge to the outside world, laid bare for this stranger. A simple truth I omit from day to day, refusing to give it any power. Shae's shoulders seem to sag under the weight, as if he is attempting to shoulder part of the burden for me.

"Well, I'm here every mornin', and will be for a few more weeks, if ye need to bend an ear." The sincerity in his kind face threatens to make a leak to spring from my traitorous eyes.

"That is awfully nice of you, but I'm sure you have more important matters to attend to than listening to some depressed stranger's babbling." I scoff, my breath quickly sucking back as I realize I just admitted my depression out loud.

"Consider me happy to return the favor, payin' it forward as ye all like to say over here. My mum was ripped away from us years ago by breast cancer. If it wasn't for the kind ears of a few friends, I don't know what I would have become." Pain and grief flit over his handsome features before settling back into his compassionate composure.

"I am sorry to hear that, Mr. MacCain." I truly am. I don't wish this hell upon my worst enemy.

"Please, call me Shae."

"Is that short for Shamus or something?" I attempt in good humor, wanting to steer the conversation far away from the black shroud that surrounds my husband's diagnosis.

"No, just Shae. My mum was a bit of rebel in that sort." He winks. "Now, I must be off to my next meetin'. See ye here tomorrow? I want to hear how yer students moaned and groaned when ye delivered that stack of horse shite back to them." He chuckles and stands, smoothing the wrinkles away from his suit.

"Most likely, depends on how the night goes." I sigh.

"Well, try to get some rest then. Ye can't keep carin' for him if ye don't take care of yourself." With that, he picks up his briefcase and saunters out the door.

What just happened? I feel like a total shit for momentarily entertaining another man, even it was harmless fun and a needed distraction. I have only had eyes for Jack since the day we met, freshman year of college. In truth, no matter what happens to him, that will never change. He is the other half of my heart. Shaking my head, I pack up and trek back to the hospital. When I near the front door, the first step in my journey back to reality, my heart falls heavy once more. Today, they are starting induction chemo on Jack with a new flavor of poison. They said this cycle will take close to two weeks, and it will be quite hard on him. Considering his blood counts and fevers, they thought it best that he stays put in the hospital for this entire round. Great.

I might as well sell the house we just bought and move in here. Or I could rent out Sorcha's flat considering she's happily living with Gavin now. When they came to visit, it was quite obvious they would be headed for the altar soon. No question has been popped yet, but I've never seen Sorcha so… so… in love. It used to be her, badgering me about my head-over-heels state. It's odd to be the one returning the favor for once. And let's be honest, she is a real pain in the ass. It takes a special kind of man to wrangle that in. Jack adores Gavin, too. They took to one another immediately when they first met a few weeks ago. Since then, I am pretty sure Gavin has seen more of Jack than I have of Sorcha. Sports and cars are all they seem to go round and round about, and just when I think they've talked about all that is possible within those two realms, they come up with something else.

It's been nice for Jack though. All his other buddies seemed to dissipate once his diagnosis got out. No one could act normal around him. Gavin treats him as if he is still one of the guys. Jack needs that outlet. Surely, he grows tired of my hovering and worrying. Lingering in the hall outside of Jack's room, I take a moment to brace for the day. The nurses will have already begun pre-treatment, gearing him up for the start of his round of controlled poisoning. Sending up a prayer once more, I grasp the handle and enter.

Jack is lightly snoring, and since he was up most of the night unable to sleep due to the pain, I creep over to the foldout bed alongside his and crawl in. He looks so peaceful. All I want to do is curl up next to him, kiss his face, and hold his frail body. Sensing my eyes, he peeks up and over his mound of pillows.

"Good morning, beautiful." He smiles, taking my breath away. Sneaking a hand out from the pile of blankets, he reaches for me.

Unable to resist, I crawl onto the tiny hospital bed, taking care not to bump or tug any of the tubes or wires attached to him. I take his cold hands in mine as we stare into each other eyes, our foreheads pressed together. He has such beautiful eyes. I had imagined our children with his eyes, the children we will never have. We were trying up until he got sick, both of us longing for a brood to call our own. I wanted to make a whole litter of babies with this man, but that, too, has been robbed from us.

Our future was planned out. Jack was a very successful lawyer, even at such a young age. His intelligence and drive took him higher than most. Thankfully, his firm gave him medical leave. They are also holding his job for whenever he is ready to return. Once he beats this thing, we will have to adopt, but we have every intention of having that family, one way or another. His cancer treatments have rendered him sterile. For whatever reason, Jack had them throw that in during his last round of testing. Jack had taken the news very personally, and I had shut off.

"What's on your mind, wife?" Jack kisses the tip of my nose.

"Just scared for today." It is impossible to lie to him, even if I try to at least attempt omission most days.

"Jade, it's like any other day. They will pump me full of poison, I'll throw up a bunch, you will go to work, and then come back here."

"Yeah."

"Baby, I'm sorry."

"What are you apologizing for?"

"For everything. You are a gorgeous, intelligent, kind, and loving woman who has been saddled with a pile of shit. You should be fat and pregnant, contemplating nursery colors. Not lying in a hospital bed, holding your dying husband. I feel fucking guilty as hell." You'd think those words would be full of anger, but not with Jack. He has a way of using his special outlook on life to lighten any serious load.

"Shut your mouth. Don't talk like that. You are not dying!" A sob unexpectedly rips from my chest, wracking my trembling body.

"Shhhh, Jade. You deserve the world, my darling wife. You deserve so much more than this." He drapes an arm over my side and runs his palm up and down my back.

"Why are you talking like this?" This is not like him at all.

"I am tired, Jade. I'm fucking eating out of a bag now." He gazes up to the TPN fluid hanging on the IV pole, artificial nutrition meant to go into his veins since his nausea and vomiting made tube feedings a bad option. "I'm wasting away to nothing."

His sudden change in tone from light and optimistic to this darkness tears another sob from my chest. He grabs the box of tissues from the bedside table and puts them between us, then wipes my eyes. "Jade, I am not giving up. Please know that." I silently nod and press my forehead back into his. His words sent one message, but the intonation behind them told me another— that he was. "You are the love of my life, Jade Ritter, and I don't plan on leaving you any time soon." Even as the words fall from his lips, it becomes clear that he doesn't believe them.

"You better not, Jack. I can't live without you." His face darkens on those sentiments, and he suddenly becomes serious.

"If I die, Jade, promise me you will try to move on with your life. Don't follow me into the grave."

"Jack, I—"

"Promise me!" His sudden rise in tone is pained and earnest.

"I promise I will try, Jack," I answer absently, scared by the direction of our exchange.

A knock on the door interrupts us once more, never a moment of peace to just be with my husband here in the hospital. He actually came home over the holidays, but he landed right back here a week ago.

"Sorry, love birds, but it's time to start." Angie, one of our favorite nurses, bustles in. She's carrying the yellow container marked *hazardous materials* on the front. Angie is in her sixties and has a few children of her own. She loves to chat about her family and just about everything else. But it is the way she cares for Jack that makes us love her. She doesn't give a shit when he doesn't feel like trying. She makes him fight, makes him power through, and makes him get up and keep going. She bickers with the doctors until she gets what she thinks Jack needs to be more comfortable, have his pain controlled, or help get him to eat. All the nurses and aids on this floor have been fabulous, but Angie and a few others stand out.

I get up and shuffle out of her way, then begin to fold up my bed to make more room as she bustles about. She gowns up, readying to plug up the chemo to my husband's withering form. It's not long before another nurse joins her to dual check and sign off the therapy before it is locked and loaded into his port. When I settle into the recliner across from Jack, I can't take my eyes off the staff and each ceremonious step they take. Angie chats with Jack, educating him on the new treatment and reminding him of the side effects as they go. I can't hear them because my mind has traveled down a dark and desolate path—a life without Jack is just not one I think I can bear.

Chapter 3

Jade

The night had gone relatively okay; Jack tolerated the treatment as well as the others with the exception of his pain becoming worse. His body became riddled with tumors over the last month, and the subsequent pain is a never-ending battle. They ended up putting him on a PCA pump of fentanyl last night, and that seemed to help him get a little rest. I almost didn't leave to come to the coffee shop this morning, but Bob, our favorite night nurse who is just as tough as Angie, kicked me out and said I needed to go recharge. Sorcha was coming by for lunch today, so that also brought us something to look forward to. I have missed our Sunday "Linner" with all of our friends for a month now, and I have refused most of their offers to come and visit. I can't handle any more sympathy right now.

Ordering my favorite mocha, I look around and find the place packed already. It's hard to tell, but it seems someone has taken my spot as well. Sighing, I take my cup from the barista and mosey over in hope that I am wrong. Nope, it is taken. Upset but trying to hide it, I glance around and see an empty chair by the window, the one with barely any table space that guaranteed coffee would be the only thing I would be able to accomplish.

"Jade? Where are ye going?" Shae's deep voice clambers through my haze as I look down in surprise.

"Oh, you saved my table?"

"Yeah, place was fillin' up fast." He motions for me to sit down. "Ye don't look like ye slept much, lass." His eyes are full of concern. Which is odd as we've just met and are strangers at best.

"Rough night. He started a new treatment yesterday." The world seems to box me in and push me down as I drift off into thought.

"Well, then I should probably start by telling you what we found yesterday." A wicked gleam sparks in his heart-stopping eyes.

He excitedly continues on, explaining in depth about the new architectural finds in the old church, as well as some artwork hidden behind a plaster wall. His enthusiasm and vivid descriptions quickly pull me from the swirling darkness. Soon, I find butterflies of excitement fluttering within me as he tells me about the paintings that have been hidden for at least a hundred years. Before long, his vibrant and animated storytelling even manages to coax a chuckle from me when he describes how the curator almost had a heart attack over the discovery. His facial expressions and hand gestures are Academy Award worthy.

And that is exactly how Shae MacCain, in the span of a few moments, ends up saving me from myself on that murky morning, and every other one, that week. Sure, he is devastatingly attractive, but that's not what I saw. It is his vibrancy and passion for art that attracts me, holds me with its hooks, and syphons my depression away.

By Saturday morning, I have a spring back in my step as I bound up the stairs, ready to debate some art or world topic or hear more about his adventures around the world. Never was he more than a gentleman; never was he inappropriate in the slightest. He asked after Jack occasionally, but he quickly changed the subject when he saw how it affected me. Somehow, he understood that he was paying it forward by distracting me, reminding me of what drove me outside of Jack. Shae was fastening a safety line I didn't know I needed. It was something not even my own friends or family could manage, but somehow, Shae had masterfully succeeded without me even realizing it.

"Here Jade, sit, I must tell ye about the email my father sent. That man is a straight nutter." He motions toward the empty seat across from him. Shae has even ordered my mocha and has it ready for me. He eagerly starts at the top, his need to vent it out evident as he hurries on.

Our budding friendship is a welcome relief. It doesn't take long before his story about his dad's antics leads into him opening up about his childhood in Scotland. We quickly bond over our similar parents, although mine are way more hippy than his could ever be.

"Shae, I doubt your dad is as crazy as my parents. I mean, come on. They named all of their children after precious stones, we rarely saw them with clothes on unless we had company, and the neighbors constantly complained that our edible garden was getting too big and intruding into their yards."

Shae laughs hysterically. "Yeah, okay, lass, ye win. Mine had the decency to wear clothes, thank the Lord for that." He sips his cup and sets it down, looking more serious all of a sudden. "Jade, tell me more about Jack. How is he doing?"

How did he know to ask that, right now, on this day of all days? The promise of the distraction he could offer was all I wanted when I came. It's not like he hasn't asked before, but why today? It feels as if the wind has been sucked out of the room, the mask of complacency falling away to the turmoil of the night. "He's... it's..." I begin to bawl. Shae had taken me completely off guard with a simple, common question. But I have become so comfortable around him that it didn't take much. This man has disarmed me in our short friendship. People begin to stare, but Shae isn't fazed. He takes out a handkerchief and hands it over. "I'm sorry." I sniff as I attempt to stop the waterworks.

"For the love of God, woman, don't be sorry," he exclaims and worriedly takes me in.

"It's not going well, Shae. He's not well. He's the love of my life, and he's dying." Ashamed of my behavior and wavering strength, I quickly stand and grab my bag. "I'm sorry; I can't be seen like this in here. I'll see you Monday, okay?" Sunday was the day all of our families came to visit, so my reprieve would have to wait until Monday. I make my way out of the shop and begin to walk to the park, in need of the distance between me and, well, people. Quickly finding a bench not far off, I sit in the cold, hoping it will numb me completely and allow me to get it together. As the biting chill stiffens my face, a leather-gloved hand with a to-go cup enters my periphery.

"Ye forgot yer coffee." I take the cup in surprise and watch Shae come around the bench to sit next to me. "Ye should ne'er be ashamed of yer emotions. Losin' someone ye love is no easy thin'."

"We had our whole lives planned, newlyweds and all. And now, I have this heavy pit in my stomach that says he isn't going to last the week." There, I had spoken it aloud. My fears, my suspicions, and my doubts.

"That's between Jack and the man upstairs, Jade." Shae's own grief over his mother shadows his face as his broad shoulders sag.

"Yeah, but I am not an idiot. The man lying in that bed is not my Jack. Cancer, the fucking beast, has stolen him from me, without my permission. I didn't ask for this, and Jack certainly didn't do a goddamn thing to deserve such a sentence!" I scream and collapse forward, my head into my hands. Why can't I get just a minute to breathe? I can't fucking breathe. Just as the world feels as if it is sucking me into an inky black oblivion, a strong, warm hand begins to circle my back, attempting to comfort me. The contact startles me, soothes me, and makes me feel guilty as hell all at the same time. Shae had become a friend, nothing more, and he hadn't so much as touched my hand until now. He is nothing but a gentleman and now a confidant in a world where no one close to me seems to understand. But my relishing in the connection makes me hate myself. I am not allowed comfort; I don't deserve it... that should only be for Jack. If Jack is suffering, then I should be, too. I scoot away from Shae. He takes the hint and retracts his arm.

"I should go. I should be by his side. Thank you for the coffee, Shae." I get up in a hurried frenzy. The bay breeze washes over me, the salt in the air kissing my senses. It chills me to the bone, providing me the needed cold to buck up and get on with it.

"See you Monday, Jade." His own sorrow hangs like a cloud in the air behind me. I refuse to make eye contact for fear of losing it again and not being able to tear myself away from the pillar of comfort he offers.

∞

Monday came and went. Shae and I continued our banter and lighthearted talks. All awkwardness had quickly passed, and our budding friendship resumed. Taking a few hours every morning to step away from that hospital room gave me the recharge and strength I needed to spend the other twenty-something fighting alongside Jack. I took leave last week and handed over my class to a substitute when it became apparent that this round of chemo was going to be very different. I was too afraid to leave Jack's side to teach, and I couldn't focus long enough to give my students what they deserved. On Friday, the last day of treatment in this cycle for Jack, the walls finally closed in and the world ripped apart at the seams in a bloody mess.

Blackness has shrouded and stifled the simple need to exist. My beating heart is now still within my chest. I can feel the contorted mass of muscle there. It's inside of me, straining and struggling in a searing attempt to find its rhythm again, but it can't. The low hum of voices fades in and out, strange faces come and go in metamorphic phases, but nothing makes sense. I don't even understand this agonizing pain undoing me from the inside out, let alone what my eyes are seeing as I clutch my chest, trying to hold my bits and pieces together. The hazy outline of a person in front of me is saying his heart has stopped. The whirlwind of staff swarming into the room behind the talking head attempting to snap me out of the state of horror is proof enough that something is wrong. The minute the monitors sounded in alarm, I had been ripped from sleep and quickly moved against the back wall, and the team began to attempt to seize Jack from the clutches of death.

Is this just a bad dream? Bodies everywhere moving in slow motion—noise, sound, yelling, and fighting for my Jack. Incessant sounds buzzing in and out of my ears. Can't they all just slow down for a minute so I can get a grasp on what is going on? I just need a minute to figure out how to breathe again. One deep breath—that's all I require to be what Jack needs.

A doctor's face comes into view. He asks if I want them to continue and do I understand what is happening… I nod, completely removed from myself. *We have to keep fighting, baby. Please hold on for me. I am almost back together to be what you need.* Panic begins to set an icy, steel grip around me in the face of possible loss.

And that's when the blood begins to bubble and spray from his mouth. It starts as a small trickle, creeping down the crease of his lips, seemingly harmless. As the nurse positioned over his chest pushes down, the trickle gives way to a gush, a floodgate now open. It's mesmerizing in a macabre, twisted fashion. Push down, blood comes out. No one seems to care as they continue to pound on his chest. I'm staring blindly, my mind blank to what this really means. His body continues to lay slack, lifeless, under the compressions. More shouting, more alarms, more voices yelling for supplies. But all I can see is his slack jaw, his lifeless flopping, and so much blood. He swore he would never leave me; he swore we would be together. He swore it, so none of this can be real.

Never have I felt so alone, here in his hospital room full of people. Strangers… the world has become nothing but strangers. They continue to shout orders. Now a tube is being put down his throat so they can artificially pump air into him. Someone yells that they think a heartbeat has come back, and they pause, and the line falls into a weird pattern again. More people, more shouting, more drugs being slammed into him as I hold myself and try to grasp if this is a sick dream or reality. Jack wouldn't want all this. It's been forever, but still nothing is working. Anger finally rips me from the hazy state.

"Stop! Stop it right now." I hear the words screamed in a voice that sounds a lot like mine. The room stills, and the same doctor's face comes into view.

"Do you understand what that means?" The face is full of sorrow, despite the sweat beading on his face.

"Yes, you will stop and let him pass. Nothing is working. He wouldn't want the tubes. He made me promise there would be no tubes. Please stop doing this to him," I yell. I run from my spot on the wall and fling myself onto the raised bed, right into the pile of tossed syringes, hot, sticky red fluid, and wires.

"It's okay, baby. I love you. Go on home to the man upstairs if you need to. No more of this, baby. You did all that you could." And as if he understands, the beeping that indicated his weak heart's attempt to beat in that funny rhythm becomes distant, weak, until it falls flat and the room begins to empty. Sobs rip from my chest as I grip and clutch in desperation at the empty vessel that once held the love of my life. Time loses all meaning. All I can hear are the crazy, guttural bellows stemming from my own broken body.

After a while, Bob, a familiar face, steps up to the bed as more pain violently washes through my body on a relentless attempt to take me down so that I can ascend and be with Jack. At least, that is what I am hoping for. Anything that hurts this bad has the end game of certain death.

"Jade, honey, let us clean him up please," Bob's gentle voice coos. He rests a hand on my shaking shoulder.

"Bob, I don't fucking give a shit. Please leave us be." He nods, finishes turning off the godforsaken alarms, and gives me my peace.

Alarms, people, noise… so much noise. An hour passes before I stumble from the hospital room to tell Bob I'll back to collect our things in a few. The world seems tilted on its axis. Nothing makes sense. I need a fucking cup of coffee and five minutes to think about how I will pack up our belongings. It can't be hard. People do this every day. *Get it together, Jade. Ya just put the shit in a bag and take it to your now-empty home.*

I cross the street in what feels like slow motion, not seeing the oncoming traffic. Actually, I see it, but I just don't care. I don't care about anything. So what if the horns are sounding for me to move out of the way? So many fast-moving vehicles. This city is so damn crowded. They can all just fucking go to hell. Fuck it. Fuck this world, and fuck everything! I raise my arms, welcoming the oncoming semi barreling down the street. I want it to take me to Jack. As the sweet surrender of what I am committing myself to do consumes me, a brute force moving faster than I can comprehend runs into me from the side, knocking me out of the wondrous arms of certain death.

I land in a heap on sidewalk, the concrete biting into my back as my head cracks against something cold. My vision blurs as pain envelops me. There is a heft weighing me down, digging into my diaphragm and making breathing nearly impossible as my automatic reflexes struggle in little gasps. Instead of fighting it, I relax into it, praying it will get heavier and end my miserable life. My head swims as the deprivation sets in, and my lungs burn, begging for a taste of oxygen. The weight quickly shifts off me. Air rushes into my chest as my body greedily takes what it needs, against my will. Distorted faces come into view, dancing around as I hear my name being yelled in the distance. Four faces circle above me… Sorcha, Gavin, Shae and… *Jack*? I see his warm, loving eyes settle on me in concern, and his lips begin to mouth something. I can't quite make it out, but I try. His lips move again in an "I love you" fashion before he fades away, and Sorcha's face comes inches within mine.

"Jack! Don't leave me. Please, God. Oh God, *no*," I scream, my hand rising to try to clutch him to me.

"Shh, Jade. Jack is back at the hospital. What were you thinking, you crazy bitch?" Sorcha's hand caresses my face as she looks into my eyes. Her other hand comes to settle over the top of mine that has her jacket in a death grip.

"He's gone, Sor. He's gone. So much blood." I weep as sobs wrack my body, and she pulls me into her lap.

"Oh, Jade, oh God. I am so sorry. We were just coming to see you, luv. For fuck's sake, look at you!" Sorcha begins to look me over and whips out her phone, turning on the flashlight app and checking my pupils. "How many fingers am I holding up?" Her stoic self takes over.

"Two."

"Good, keep looking here at my nose and tell me when you see my fingers come into your vision." I do as she asks and allow her to continue checking me out. She may have ditched med school to pursue her passion, but she will always be a doctor at heart. Even with trembling hands and fear imprinted on her face, she assumes the brave caretaker, always. When her hands start to poke around my shirt, I quickly remember Shae and Gavin hovering near and slap her intruding hands away.

"Sorcha, I am fine," I insist and try to sit up, a wave of faltering gravity making it difficult.

"Then where is all of this blood coming from? You are covered." She helps me into the sitting position, her hands brushing away debris from my pants.

"It's not mine. God, there was so much blood. He's dead. He's really dead." My head falls into my hands as Gavin begins crowd control, and embarrassment suffocates me as I realize the downward trickle of my rash decision. So many faces leering, judging, or pitying me. Their hushed tones poison my ears and make me wish that truck had gunned it for me.

"You stupid cunt! I almost fucking hit you!" The truck driver makes toward us, white as a ghost and shaking in fear.

"Easy there, fella, simple accident. That's all." Shae steps in the man's way, broadening his chest and blocking his view of me as I cringe in indignity. Gavin approaches the man and magically exercises his gift of situational containment. It's not long before the dude heads back to his truck after throwing me a few sideways glances. I have no clue what Gavin or Shae said, but it worked.

Thankful for that intervention, I decide it's time to get up. The city sounds of traffic and people blare into my throbbing head, and my need to cower away from it all takes the lead. Feeling as naked and vulnerable as the day I was born, I get to my feet and immediately sway.

"Whoa there, lass." Shae rushes to my side, worry etched in his beautiful face as he slips an arm around my shoulders to steady me.

"Come on, then. Let's get her to the hospital for a head CT. She may even need a few stiches on the gusher on the back of her head," Sorcha barks, the stress of it all eating away at her resolve.

"No, no, *no*! No more hospitals. Please, no!" I begin to shake and step back despite Shae's grip on me. Pissed that his hands are on me, I shove them off and begin to back away from them all.

"Jade, they really need to examine ye. I am so sorry. This is my fault, I didn't mean to push ye so hard, but that guy was speedin'," Shae pleas as he sees the hysteria setting in.

"Seriously? You are apologizing? You saved her life! I'd gladly knock her head around a few times if that meant it kept her from being roadkill," Sorcha declares incredulously as she runs a hand through her long hair and pulls in frustration.

"Babe, she doesn't want to go to the hospital. Can't you patch her up at home?" Gavin tries to rationalize with her, his accent deepening as he edges closer to me, uncertain of what I might try next.

"Gavin, I don't have those kinds of supplies, and she could really use a scan." Sorcha's forehead wrinkles, her chest reddening under the pressure of building emotions she'll never admit to.

"I will get you what you need. Okay?" She nods to him and turns her glare back on me, forcing me to freeze.

"You, you, you… *You* are on my shit list for trying a stunt like that! What the fuck would Jack say? I tell ya what he'd say—" She begins to curse frantically in Gaelic. Gavin pulls her into him, caressing her bright red cheek and whispering something in her ear. The tension in her body turns down a notch as she sniffs and nods. After she leans her cheek on Gavin's chest, her damp eyes find mind once again. My hands clutch at the parking meter near me as I try to steady my antsy feet. I've hurt too many. Maybe I should just run away and disappear. "Let's go home. You are coming home with us, okay?"

The raw emotion in her voice daggers me. Running would hurt them even more, I can't do that. "Okay. Can we go now? Just leave all of our shit there; I don't want any of it, and I don't want to go near another fucking hospital for the rest of my life." I begin to shiver and look at the ground, not wanting to feel any more eyes on me.

"Let's get to the car, ladies. I will fetch the rest." Gavin kindly offers. I attempt to take a step forward, but my legs buckle. Strong arms catch me before lifting me up and pulling me into a firm, broad chest. I hadn't even noticed Shae working his way back over to me in my strung-out state. Gavin eyes Shae speculatively, the attention forcing me to turn my head and rest it on Shae's wool coat. Pathetic. I am utterly pathetic. I never did tell either of them about my new friend, and suddenly, here he is in the thick of it. Wait, this is so fucking wrong.

"Put me down, Shae," I forcibly grit, trying to wiggle out of his arms.

"No, lass, ye are in no shape. I'll be puttin' ye in the back of their car," he declares, sounding past done with my attempt to push everyone away.

"I said put me down. I can't do this. I can't be around any of you. I don't deserve any of it! You should have just let me die!" A panic-stricken sob tears through me as I beat on his chest in frustration. Steel arms pin me closer, the fibers of his coat biting into my cheek as I fight him.

"I got ye," Shae whispers as he slowly follows Gavin and Sorcha to the car, taking my abuse without another word as I wail and struggle against his vice grip. After a few minutes, I lose the strength to fight as my adrenaline slows, and I turn my head to look at the solemn faces of my comrades. The broken hearts are evident; their attempts to hold it together for me through their own pain of loss is loud and clear. The last little hiccup escapes me as I realize my selfishness. Sorcha casts a long glance over her shoulder before nodding to me and taking Gavin's hand.

"I can walk. I'm not an invalid. Put me down, Shae," I weakly attempt one last time, mortified of my actions.

"Says the one who just tried to walk in front of a semi. Hush up." His attempt at a grin eases my shame. At this point, it doesn't matter anyway. We reach the car. Shae deposits me into the back of Gavin's black sedan, taking care not to bump me along the way. Sorcha clambers in right next to me, pinning me in. My head drops to her shoulder as the door closes, and I see the two men talking as they walk through the parking lot of the hospital to retrieve the frivolous things that I really don't want. They are going to carry through with it despite what they just witnessed me do. Why do they even bother? It's all tainted with memories I don't want.

"Jade, lovey, look at me." I peer into her brilliant green eyes, and my own mismatched ones well with silent tears once more.

Sorcha has been my best friend since we were young, and even though I have shut out the rest of the group since just past the New Year, she remains the one person who can get through to me— see the real me past all the hurt, pain, and betrayal.

"Friend, it's not your fault. None of this is your fault. Do you hear me?" I nod, and again rest my head on her shoulder. She strokes my hair. "This is just one of those inexplicable motherfucking things that happens that is out of our control. You did everything right. You fought by his side, you gave all that you had to give, and, while death still came, everything you did was enough."

Guilt rips through me as I pick myself apart. "No, Sor, I should've quit going to work a lot sooner. I should have stopped going to the coffee shop in the mornings. That is time I could have been with him that I wasted."

"No, that was time you both needed apart so that you could appreciate your time together that much more."

"I never gave him the baby he wanted either." I don't know where that came from. I guess both of us being infertile has been bothering me more than I thought. He wanted a baby so bad; I failed him at that too.

"Stop it, it wasn't meant to be. Could you imagine? Dealing with this and a child?'

"It would have given me something to live for—a piece of him. I've got nothing left."

"Bullshit. You have Ruby, your parents, and hello… Me for God's sakes!"

"He was my world." Depression seats itself deep within my soul as I begin to feel the sticky grey sadness settle around me like a heavy chain mail, altering me permanently.

"What about your art?" My heart sings at the brief thought before the enveloping darkness cuts that happiness out at the knees.

"I don't know if I will ever have the heart for that again." Sorcha huffs, leans to grab her purse, pulls out a packet of tissues, and begins to wipes my eyes.

"Oh, my sweet Jade, only time will tell. For right now, let's just focus on getting you home and tucked in."

Home is funny word. Nothing and nowhere felt like that anymore. Jack was my home. Thoughts of Shae drift by, and I realize that I haven't said much to my knight-in-shining armor who has just seen me at my worst.

"Damn it, what am I going to do about Shae? I don't want him coming back with us to the house. He's just an acquaintance, and he doesn't need to bother himself with me."

"Who is he really, Jade?" Sorcha asks in a kind tone, no judgment at all.

"He's someone I met at the coffee house. I'd chat with him, nothing more."

"Well, he's got impeccable timing, thank the Lord for that!"

"I hate to say it, but I am not sorry I tried to kill myself. I don't want to live anymore, yet I feel like now I have to." My tears slow as the reverence sings through my words.

"Love, I can only imagine what you are going through. We will just keep that bit to ourselves and not share with the rest of our lot or your family. You are going to feel and go through whatever you need to, and I will be there to support you... and slap the shit out of you if you try to peace out on me any time soon."

"It's a deal."

It doesn't take long before the men return, and an overwhelming need to justify myself to Shae forces me out of the backseat as they place my bags into the trunk.

"Thank you, guys. Gavin, could you give us a minute?" Gavin nods and slips into the driver's seat, his eyes heavy on us from the rearview mirror.

Shae stands there with his hands in his pockets, gazing at me with so much sympathy. It becomes too much. "Shae, thank you. For everything. I am so sorry you had your morning taken up with all this nonsense. I am sorry you had to see that—" I motion to the street, not wanting to give the ordeal more power or justification with words.

"Jade, I'd do it again in a heartbeat. This is more than one person should ever have to deal with, and I am so very sorry for yer loss." His blue eyes are sincere as his hands slip into the pockets of his heavy jacket.

"Please, stop. I can't handle all the sympathy. It's too much."

"Aye, that I can also understand."

"You've been wonderful. Thank you for taking the time to give me something else to focus on, even it was only for just a few minutes a day. I feel guilty as hell for it right now, wrong somehow. Maybe someday I will look at it differently." I wrap my arms around myself against the chilly, arctic breeze.

"The time with ye helped me as well, Jade. Now, I suggest ye get back in that car and warm up. Ye've got two who love ye fiercely right there." He opens the back door for me, motioning for me to get in.

"Guess this is the end of the line for our coffee breaks." I rub my arm, trying to warm up.

"Guess so, until we meet again. Take care of yerself, lass, and ne'er forget that fire of yers that burned me a time or two when I dared to cross yer choices in brush strokes." Humor lights his eyes when I offer a weak smile.

"Bye, Shae. Good luck on the rest of your projects." I get in, and he closes the door for me. He smiles, raising a hand in a slight wave and stepping back.

With that, we drive off, Shae in the rearview mirror and the cold, grey sky before us. A part I don't care to acknowledge will really miss our lighthearted mornings spent over steaming cups of therapy. Thinking back to all of those chats, I am reminded of something outside of my life with Jack, a piece of myself I had almost forgotten about when Jack's diagnosis consumed us. I had let cancer swallow my entire life, my entire being. My short time with Shae really did fasten a little life vest around me.

Suddenly, as we drive toward the coast and the sun sets in the sky, the thought of living another day seems almost doable in spite of the gut-wrenching pain coursing through me. Jack made me promise I would go on without him, a promise I'd absently made, and I owed it to him to try to fulfill it.

∞

I stand at the edge of the shore, the frigid waves lapping at my bare feet. I huddle tightly under my shawl.

"You ready, baby girl?" Samuel asks as Reed steps up and takes his hand, and Molly nestles in close to them.

"Yeah." My hands begin to shake when uncap the urn.

"Here, let me get that." Breonna takes the lid from my hand. It's all I can do not to thrust the rest of the urn at her as well.

Dozens of Japanese lanterns light up the night as Jack's friends and family gather at the edge of the sea. With these lanterns, we are returning our beloved to nature in a ceremonious manner. I peer down into the steel container at the remnants left behind of the great man they once composed. I don't want to let go of these ashes; I don't want to return him to the sea that he loved. I want to hold on to what is left of him forever.

But that is not what he would have wanted. He made me have this conversation after his first round of chemo, forced me to speak of the unspeakable… his end-of-life wishes. Jack loved the sea. We spent most summer days lounging by it or boating. He used to tell me all the time that we would sail around the world, just the two of us, once our kids were grown.

Once more, tears flow freely as my lips press to the side of the biting cold metal. Whispering my undying love for the last time, I promptly turn it upside down before I change my mind, allowing him to spill into the water. The light ocean breeze caresses me before sweeping in and carrying the last of his lingering ashes away. I hug the now-empty urn tightly to my shaking figure as people slowly step up from behind me. One by one, they all take a moment to honor Jack, place their lanterns in the water, and turn to offer condolences to his parents, who are standing near me. A few step into my personal space and attempt a hug or hand hold, but most just smile and nod, knowing how hard this is for me. Countless faces, all part of our lives in some sense, yet they all feel like strangers. After absentmindedly hugging Jack's aunt and watching as her lantern is chased out to sea, I turn to see a familiar face step through the crowd. He bends to gently place a lit, paper wonder in the water to join the mass of them.

"Shae?" My eyes go wide in surprise.

"I had to say good bye before I leave." He promptly stands at the sound of my voice, steps back, and takes me in.

"How did you know—"

"Yer friends are quite resourceful, tracked me down and invited me." He winks and nods toward Gavin.

My heart swells at the gesture and at seeing his face. I really have missed our chats over the last week. Simple conversations about so many things that, in their own way, had become a comfort.

"Thank you for coming, Shae. I really mean that." My whole being is drawn to him, screaming and yelling at me to let him wrap me up in his arms, but I ignore it.

"You take care of yourself." He attempts to comfort the sadness within me with a chaste hug, which I allow. Warmth radiates off him. Thankfully, it doesn't feel awkward. With a sly smile, he bows his head, shoves his hands into the pockets of his slacks, and strolls back down the path.

My heart squeezes at the sight of him leaving, and I find myself walking down the path behind him. Hundreds of lanterns now dot the blacked sea of the coastline in honor of Jack. A beautiful, hopeful metaphor sweeps through the powerful, churning body of water, lighting it in a poetic fashion. As the crowd falls silent, many slowly embrace one another as they look on, the sounds of the ocean adding to the hypnotic and emotional effect.

"Shae, wait up." I struggle to keep up with his long strides.

He turns around in surprise.

"I can't believe you actually came," I manage in a breathy billow of cold air

"Why wouldn't I?"

"Come to the funeral of a stranger's dead husband? It doesn't sound like my idea of a good time." I sarcastically admonish.

"I came to the funeral of my friend's deceased husband. We may have not had the privilege of knowin' each other long, but I came to cherish those conversations. Helped me with some of my own baggage. My intention was to help someone in need, and, in turn, ye helped me."

"Really? You never mentioned—"

"No need. It is old stuff. It didn't fit with the time." His gaze wistfully darts out to the show that the lanterns are performing in the tide.

"Would have been nice to know I wasn't the only one hurting." It falls out of my mouth before I have a chance to reconsider.

"Jade, in life, ye never know what another is battling or the miles they have walked." His head cocks as his eyes thoughtfully come to rest on mine.

Shit. I feel like a real ass now. "Oh, I didn't mean… crap. I am sorry for being so self-involved."

"Ye had every right to be. I really wish ye the best."

"Thank you. You actually are leaving?"

"Aye. Gotta hop back across the pond and get back to the growin' pile of work." He shrugs and looks away.

Is this the part where I remind him to use the email address I gave him? "Thank you again, Shae."

"Twas nothing. Bye, sweet Jade." He gives me a tight smile and turns to amble up the beach path, into the darkness.

Shaking off the odd feelings niggling at the fringes of my emotions, I turn around and head back to the gathering. Shoulder to shoulder with my sister Ruby and Sorcha, I gaze out at the sight before us. Jack would have very much approved. The tiny lanterns rocked and swayed as the ocean waves pulled them out further, lighting up a part of the night that would otherwise be black. Silent tears of grief roll down my cheeks. I've never cried this much in my life, and I pray I never cry this much ever again.

We each stand on the cold beach, breaths puffing little clouds. I imagine everyone is internally battling with fond memories and a sense of overwhelming, all-consuming grief.

Goodbye, my love. May God keep you well and may your selfless soul never suffer another single second.

Shae

It has been utter agony, knowing the pain she is suffering and not being close enough to absorb some of it from her. The lass stole my heart from day one, but it's not like I was ever going to act on it. I'm not a complete asshole. Although, I am beginning to question that. What kind of man falls for a dying man's wife in her lowest moment? But how could I not? She is the very definition of perfection—passionate, intelligent, and witty. She is grace with a touch of fire, not to mention the bonniest lass I've ever seen. Faodail is a good word from back home for it, a very rare find indeed.

As I agonizingly turn from her once more on this desolate, sandy path, leaving the glowing tribute now fanning out over the sea, my mind flits over the first day I saw her. It was a dreich day, thunder and rain coming from all about as she rushed in, oblivious to anything around her but the task at hand. I stood against the wall as she walked in a haze, fumbling a bit as she sat down to meticulously arrange her makeshift workspace. Finally finding a seat just across from her, I sat transfixed, completely mesmerized by the creature before me. The memory that sits freshest in my mind, however, is the moment she felt my eyes on her. She had turned the loveliest shade of pink that I have ever seen as our eyes briefly met. Her blonde waves of hair fell angelically around her face, and her rosy lips formed a pout as the subtle gray skies backlit her through the window. If I hadn't known better, I would have believed her to truly be an angel. In that instant, we shared a connection that could not be dulled by space, time, or circumstance. In the next, she began to ferret away broken pieces of my heart for her own keeping, a collection that only grew with the weeks to come.

And now I leave her in the arms of sorrow, surrounded by those she loves, yet strangers all the same. She had made it clear a time or two how alone she felt. Alas, no one can truly understand that level of heartbreak and loss unless they've suffered through it. The loss of my mum was hard, but I don't think it compares to that of losing a spouse so young.

One thing is certain, walking away from her has to be the hardest thing I've ever done. All I want to do is to wrap her in my arms and hold her through it, remind her of her strength, and all the parts in life worth living for. But I can't be the salve to her aching wounds. She has to properly grieve this on her own. I will be of no use in that process except to prolong, distract, or inhibit. Lord, I pray that one day I can become the man she needs and that our paths will cross again.

Fighting the need to turn back around with everything I possess, I trek back to my car in my own cloud of despair. Climbing into the driver's seat, I look out over the bay at the hundreds of twinkling lights now crowding the cove in which they began their journey out to sea, carrying the legacy of a well-loved man. How big of a bastard am I for being jealous of such a man? I should be happy for him that he got to experience all that he had in such a short time, including loving the amazing woman I long for. Perhaps, in time, I'll realize this has all been an infatuation, and it will pass. Onward and upward, I suppose.

Chapter 4

Jade

One year later.

"Jade! Please don't go. Stay here and let's have Devon look at your paintings." Sorcha's palm comes down in a startling fashion on the Formica tabletop at our favorite diner. We are all gathered here for our Sunday "Linner." None of us could ever get our act together before two on a Sunday, hence the need for a Linner instead of a brunch.

"Sorcha, that is very kind of you, but I need to do this for myself." I coolly lean back and ignore her outburst.

"Travel around the UK for weeks by yourself? Pure and utter straight crazy." Her bottom lip pouts as she slouches back and crossing her arms over her chest like a petulant child.

"She's right. We could take turns coming with you," Breonna offers, and Molly, Ben, and Samuel all nod in agreement.

I knew breaking the news to them would be hard. "Guys, this isn't an existential crisis. I didn't take a job over there or anything. I've sold off everything and have been living in Sorcha's old studio. The spring semester just ended, and I have the entire summer to do something for myself. I need to do this for my healing process. I've been a shell since Jack. I need to find myself." I had practiced the speech a million times over in the bathroom mirror before coming, yet it seems quite foreign in the moment.

"For fuck's sake, take some long and meaningful walks around the city. That will help you find yourself, and plenty of trouble if need be," Sorcha mutters, and then stuffs a bite of pancake into her mouth.

"I think it's a great idea, Jade." Molly bobs her head and tries to hide her own sadness.

"Thanks, Molly."

"Can Gavin set you up with some spy shit for safety?" Samuel frets in true male form.

"I don't know what he did to my phone, but I can apparently call any of you at any time. Text too." I had told Gavin of my plans a few days ago; he had been the only one to know. The man has become like the big brother I never knew I wanted.

That seems to satisfy all of them, with the exception of Sorcha, who puts two and two together and is not happy that her man knew before she did. She arches her brow and opens her mouth, but I cut her off. "Sor, you are getting ready to go on a gallery tour around Europe in the fall. You will get your turn to hop a plane," I say in good humor.

"That's not it and you know it."

"I will be fine. I really will." After my attempt to tango with a semi, she has been on me like a fly on shit. She is afraid I am going to try something stupid once over there. She couldn't be farther from the truth. I feel driven to do this. To go look for myself. I need to throw my shell of a self completely out of my comfort zone and get to know Jade all over again. I've never really been alone. This will be good for me.

"Just you all promise me something—no weddings until I get back." I wink. Sorcha almost chokes on her eggs, and a prompt scowl to cross her face. Everyone laughs. She's madly in love, but the thought of marriage remains more than she can take. "Sorcha, you are basically married anyway." She turns bright pink before shaking her head and glaring at the rest of us as we chuckle.

"All right, if she tries to run for the altar, or if any of us do for that matter, I'll see to it personally that they wait," Samuel promises, his dark blue eyes lighting up. Ben, Molly, and Breonna shake their heads and offer kind words of encouragement. Despite never wanting anything to do with another man, I remain a romantic at heart and will always be a sucker for it. Looks like a lifetime of cats, B-movies, and late-night dates with Ben and Jerry's from here on out. That doesn't seem so bad. I've had my once-in-a-lifetime love. Most never even get that.

"When do you leave?" Ben's kind voice snakes out through the clatter of the group digging into their food.

"Tomorrow."

Sorcha looks as if her eyes are going to bug out of her head. Where was Gavin when you needed him to tame the fiery little beast? She slams her coffee down and gets up. "Bathroom," she mumbles over her shoulder and stalks off. Samuel gives me a sideways glance and moves to go after her. He and his Dom self are usually better at stepping in when she gets like this.

"I got it, Samuel." I had expected her to take this hard. It was a shit move to not even tell her that I was planning it. But I knew how she would act. She doesn't have an issue with the fact that I was going, it was that she was worried sick over me going alone. And she would miss me, but not nearly as much as I would miss her. We've spent more time together over the last twelve months than we had in years. Once we finished college, our quality time together diminished. We talked almost every day, but it was never the same as curling up together with a bottle of wine and a movie or going shopping together. All of us have spent more time together over the last year. Samuel and Reed took me out to dinner frequently, I helped Breonna and my sister Ruby with their kids quite a bit, and even Ben and his darling husband managed to weasel me out of the house once in a while. Molly has even become my new walking buddy. We both detest running and left that to Sorcha, but our evening walks proved quite healthy. They have all come together to make sure I am taken care of and healthy. I couldn't ask for a better bunch, but I feel smothered. I went from living at home with one big, crazy family to college. Jack and I fell in love the first semester of school, and I haven't been alone since. It's time.

Pushing back the door to the ladies' room, I peer in to find my bestie drying her red, puffy eyes in the bathroom. Unused to seeing fluid leaking from her face, I am a little taken aback as guilt rips through me. Sorcha rarely cries, and I mean almost never. She gets hotheaded and worked up. That's basically her version of crying.

"Shit, Sor, if I had known you'd be this torn up, I would have given you a bit of notice," I say as I make my way to her and throw an arm around her slender waist, pulling her in close to my side.

"Ya think?" She blows her nose hard, making her big, green eyes appear even larger.

"Is everything okay?" Something else is up.

"Uh...yes! My bestie is leaving me, I just found out I'm pregnant, and I can't be pregnant! I haven't told Gavin, neither of us wants kids, and now you are leaving. How am I supposed to deal with this?" The waterworks turn on full blast as she pulls away and throws her arms up in a fury. Yeah, pregnancy hormones. That explains it. Sadness tugs at my heart, reflecting my own desires and struggles from another lifetime, but I tuck it away and focus.

"Sor, love, come on. Gavin is going to be ecstatic. It will all be okay." My hip comes to rest against the bathroom counter as my arms move around my center, protecting me from any pain that may come from my emotions.

"I can't have a baby, Jade."

"Sor, stop talking crazy. You are both working professionals, and this will be great."

"I work half naked at a bar and like to get my ass spanked. How fucking healthy is that?" She snorts and grabs another paper towel to mop her face.

"Sor, you don't have to work at the bar at all, and you know it. Your photography has taken off. And aside from having to put a lock on that damn room of yours, the kid will be fine."

Sorcha blows her nose heavily again. "I am too young to have a kid, Jade." She sniffs and turns away from the mirror, disgusted with herself.

"Sor, you are thirty-one, looking down the barrel of thirty-two. It's not like you are twenty-one." She makes an ew face as we both share a moment of our private joke. Every time we go out and are around twenty-somethings, we say a silent prayer that we are in our thirties. "Talk to your man." I wipe a runaway streak of mascara off her cheek with the pad of my thumb. "Since when have you ever been afraid of anything?" I tease.

"Who says I am afraid?" Her Irish pride perks.

"Not me, clearly." I wink at her.

"That's what I thought. Now, can you tell Gavin?" She bumps her hips into mine and gives me a big hug.

"Not a chance." I giggle. That man may be like a brother, but he still scares the shit out of me.

"Please, don't say anything to them. If they find out before Gavin, I won't be able to sit straight for months." Her eyes go wide again at the thought.

"My lips are sealed. Oh, God, I can't believe I am going to miss out on Bre's face when she finds out!" I squeal and wrap my arms around her even tighter. Breonna has been waiting on this moment since before she had kids herself. The woman is going to fuss over Sorcha worse than their own mother will.

"You are going to have to clean up that face a little better if you don't want her to see right through you." I snicker as I ease back to take a better look at her. God, I am so happy for them. Aside from needing to clean up her mouth, she is going to make one hell of a mother. She is amazing, smart, and full of passion for life. And Lord help her, Gavin is going to be quite overprotective. She'll be lucky if she is allowed to walk on her own for nine months. Have I mentioned how much she hates that too? Oh, this will be grand. Thankfully, I am only gone for part of the summer. There will still be a front-row seat waiting for me as soon as I get back.

Sorcha attempts to fix her makeup and pinch her cheeks to put some color in them, but she does a piss-poor job seeing that her purse is back at the table. After a few minutes, she gives up with a massive shrug, as if she is subconsciously trying to accept her fate, and we head back.

About a foot away from the table, Breonna looks up and locks onto Sorcha, causing me to instinctively wait for the smoke to come as she assesses us.

"You all took long enough," Breonna begins, eyes trained like hunter.

"Sorry, we just had to hash some things out." I try to throw off the bloodhound, but I know it's pointless.

"I call bullshit," Breonna declares as the others all stare at her, waiting for the other shoe to drop.

Sorcha plays it off and sits down next to Samuel as I scoot in next to Molly. None of us have our significant others here; this is our time. I mean, none of them have theirs. Staving off my own dampening eyes, I attempt to act as if nothing is up. Amazing how just when you think things like that can't hurt you anymore, they perk their little tails up and remind you.

"Sorcha?" Breonna questions, and Sor looks up automatically, which is the wrong move.

"What, Bre?"

"Why have you been crying?" Breonna presses. We can almost see the spotlight on Sorcha as the interrogation begins.

"I am worried about Jade. Isn't that enough?" Sorcha counters.

"You never cry." After Breonna calls her bluff, the rest of us watch in silence as the trains collide.

"I am allowed to cry."

"No!"

"I'm not allowed to cry?" Sorcha mutters and starts in on her cold food.

"Only two things could make you cry…" Breonna starts. I see Sorcha's cheeks turn rosy and grab my mug, sipping away as I watch the show.

"Oh, snap." Samuel coughs.

"You're pregnant," Breonna exclaims loudly, causing everyone else to choke on the spot.

All we can do is sit back and watch. This… this right here needs to be a YouTube channel or something. Sorcha turns the shade of a beet while the whole restaurant turns to stare. In slow motion, Sorcha sucks in air, and I just wait. One—two—three—and… they erupt in an argument in a different language. I can only pick up a word or two here and there.

Sorcha and I have been friends since she shared her lunch with me back in second grade. My parents had packed homegrown stuff, all vegetarian, and I hated it. Her mum had packed her a beef stew that smelled like straight heaven and was miraculously still warm in the thermos. She saw me staring, and offered to share. I tossed my veggies in the trash, and we've been thick as thieves since. Even after all this time, through all their outbursts, I only knew a few words of her native tongue. The whole restaurant remains captivated until Sorcha slaps her hand on the table, breaking the trance. Out of all her idiosyncrasies, I wish she'd stop that particular one. It makes my heart jump out of my chest every time.

"Fine! Yes," Sorcha admits.

Breonna smiles like the Cheshire cat. "Oh. My. God. I knew it! You never eat this much. You've been a downright cow lately."

"Thanks a lot, Bre," Sorcha grumbles and places her head in her hands.

"Seriously? You won't let him put a ring on it, but sure, throw a bun in there," Samuel banters in good humor, and Molly and Ben chime in, chattering excitedly as Sorcha looks more and more like she wants to disappear.

"All right, ease up. Gavin doesn't know yet. She's going to leave here and tell him right away," I say.

"He doesn't know?" Breonna tsks.

"I just found out this morning. You are all cunts; you know that, right?" She slams her forehead onto the table.

"Oh, my. Well, you best get out of here and tend to your business, because I am calling Mum after we are done," Breonna warns her. The look on Sorcha's face is absolutely priceless. Samuel and Ben pretend to check their phones, and Molly hungrily begins to shovel the last of her food in, their happy gossip cut short.

"Bre, please, I am begging you. Let me tell, Gavin first. Please!" Sorcha very well might have a stroke here and now judging by that vein now bulging in her forehead.

"Fine, but this calls for a party!" Bre excitedly begins chatting away, to no one in particular, on her plans for another Irish shindig with lots of food.

"Bre—no! Plan the fucking baby shower, but nothing until then, okay?" Sorcha pleads as if she is begging for her life, and Bre gives her a half-sad, half-devilish grin.

"You know this means the two of you will have to get married, and I can plan that too." Bre giggles like a maniac.

In unison, we all yell "Bre!" in warning. She went too far, too fast.

"Okay, fine." Bre crosses her arms. As polished as Bre likes to think she is with her chignon and pearls, she's just as bad as her sister.

Sorcha seems to relax a bit until her phone buzzes. She returns to that lovely shade of crimson red and nervously bits her bottom lip.

"Go on, Sor. Go talk to him," I urge, knowing it's the only person in this world who can undo her in an instant.

"I don't want to miss my last day with you, Jade." She groans.

"I am only going to be gone a few weeks," I remind her, and my heart begins to ache again.

"Okay, but we will still text or talk every day, right?"

"Yes, every day, all of you if you want." We all stand and begin to hug and say our goodbyes.

It is my dream trip. I can do this. I promised Jack I would go on and live, but over the last year, I've done nothing but exist. I need to learn how to live again. In order to do that, I need to figure out the new me.

Gavin's black Acura pulls up outside of the diner, and Sorcha's face falls.

"Good luck, babe. Call me if you need me." I hug her deeply, kiss her cheek, and watch her drag ass all the way to the car. The others trail behind her. I bring up the back end, walking out after the group. As they turn one direction out the front door, I turn in the opposite. Time to finish packing and get on with this.

Chapter 5

Jade

I find it funny how being alone can scream the truth about your life. Falling into bad choices or failing at it all, whatever the difference, but maybe this was a bad idea. I've been in London for five days, and I have done more tours than I thought possible in that time. Besides the tours, I've packed my days with utter nonsense. Well, the British Museum was amazing, but the rest has just been filler. Ways to ease my glaring loneliness.

The first day was jam-packed with food and jet lag. After that, there was the thrill of being in a new place. I had spent the subsequent days bustling up and down random streets, in and out of little shops, absorbing whatever possible in-between tours. Six cities and a little of over a week in each place was the plan. It was plenty of time to gorge myself on the culture, art, and food. Too much time as it would seem. I'm already losing steam. Not knowing what to do with myself for the day, I dress and leave my hotel for a walk, hunting for inspiration.

Sitting around and waiting for the rest of my time in London to pass isn't going to do me any good. My art didn't even hold my interest, not that it has since Jack passed. The thought of pulling out my drawing pad makes me cringe. Not to mention, another minute in that hotel room, and I was about to become a liability. If I had been thinking, I would have reached out via social media through some of those travel sites and connected with locals to learn more about what to do. Gavin's family lives a few minutes away and offered to put me up, but I didn't want to impose. Perhaps I should reconsider for the rest of my trip. His brother, James, sounds like a character, and a friendly face would be nice about now.

Spying a bakery up ahead, I duck in and whip out my phone as I wait in line. The scent of croissants and coffee make my belly grumble. I message Gavin and ask for his brother's number. It feels more natural to reach out to the brother than Gavin's parents. Who am I kidding? None of it feels natural. They came out and visited Sorcha and Gavin over the holidays, but I opted out of that family gathering and holed up with my own. I probably have some awkward reputation with them already.

After I collect my treats and find a little bistro table outside, my phone chimes. Gavin has set up a time and place for me to meet James tonight. Great. I don't even get to ease into the thought; the control freak did what he does best. Perhaps socializing might actually do me some good, though.

A heavy sigh escapes me as I look around, people watching and taking in my surroundings. My heart lurches in my chest. Jack would have loved this. We talked about doing this very thing, on a trip just like this. Immersing ourselves in the food, people, and culture. I am doing all right on the food part, and some of the culture, but failing on the people aspect. It is hard to want to meet new people when all I can do is compare them to our friends and family back home and ponder what Jack would think. He was the natural social butterfly in our relationship, while I struggled with the self-involved affliction most artist have. That's not to say I can't develop attachments to others—simply that it takes longer. But when I do, it's passionately deep. And letting go is not to be taken lightly when the memories haunt you like a gothic-era painting.

I still have to stuff pillows behind my back and one in the front to hug in order to be able to sleep at night. It has been a year, and the pain has only mildly dulled. I've spent so much time thinking about Jack and what he would do, say, or think that my own opinions have embarrassingly paled. As a person, I have faded. Hence the need for this trip. I needed to feel something, do something grand… find the lost Jade instead of being wrapped up in everyone else's thoughts, emotions, and memories. Hardly ever being one for booze, I think tonight that might need to change. Apparently, James likes to enjoy himself, and maybe I should too.

∞

I hesitantly walk into the bar just outside Piccadilly Circus, my hands nervously twisting together. This seems too touristy of a place. I would have preferred something the locals frequented, but who knows what Gavin and his brother had been thinking. Before I can change my mind and head back to the hotel, a handsome, more approachable version of Gavin zeros in on me and heads over. Gavin said he sent a picture of me to James so he could find me.

"Jade, is it?" His husky voice causes my heart to speed up. I immediately chastise myself for the reaction with guilt-driven content.

"Yes. James?" I stick out my hand to formally shake his. His brown eyes are a bit darker than Gavin's, more mischievous.

Good Lord, he is straight sex on a stick. Gavin is harder. His edge distorts his devastating good looks for some. Not to mention he is like a brother and basically married to my best friend. But James? One look from him sends shivers down my spine and not the bad kind either. He takes my hand, his warm one enveloping mine.

"Pleasure to meet you. Come, let me get you a drink." He doesn't let go of my hand, rather holds it firmly as he leads me through the crowd to a table. He starts to pull out my chair, but the thought of sitting at a table with him, alone, becomes too much, and my anxiety kicks up. Pulling back, I motion for him to stop.

"Can we sit at the bar?"

He nods and takes us there, pulling out the stool for me, just like Jack used to.

"Thank you." The bar area knocks the intimacy down a slight notch.

"What'yal have?"

"Just a water." He gives me an odd look, and I suddenly hate my boring self. "What do you recommend?"

"Beer?" A rich and deep sound emanates in the form of a chuckle from his chest. "Depends on what you are after. Pimms and lemonade if you don't want beer or whiskey." The heartiness of his laugh helps me soften up. I'm sure Gavin warned him about me, about how unavailable I am. This will be just a harmless encounter.

"I don't know what the Pimms thing is, but I will try that." He promptly waves down the bar maiden and orders before turning his full attention back to me.

"You enjoying London?"

"Yeah," I chirp, but his eyes hold me, seeing right through my uneasiness. "Ugh, well, yes and no. I've loved the sights and all, but coming all this way on my own has been a little tough," I sheepishly admit. "Oh God, please don't let that get back to your brother, or I'll never hear the end of it."

"Oh hell, not to worry." He booms out another laugh as our drinks arrive. "Here, you need this, love. Bottoms up!" He pushes the drink toward me and palms his own. The collar of his button-up shifts, showing a muscular and smooth chest peeking over the top. My eyes are fixated until my cheeks warm, and I quickly avert my eyes. *Get a grip, Jade, you are married woman. No need to lust after the man.*

I sip mine. Vodka and lemonade burst over my taste buds, and my shoulders begin to lower on impact. Oh, that is good. Aside from the occasional glass of wine, I haven't really had much alcohol in the last couple of years. This damn thing tastes like a dessert. Before I know it, James is looking at me in good humor, and I realize I've inhaled the whole glass. Peering down into my glass in surprise, I roll my shoulders a few times. My nerves are notably better now.

"You'll have another then?" He smirks.

The growing scene in the pub proves hard competition with my initial, mousey state of being. "Yes, please," I timidly say, unsure of why Gavin's brother is making me feel uneasy. His tousled light brown hair, broad shoulders, dark brown eyes, high cheekbones, and dimples… he's totally someone's kid brother who is probably still in college. He could be one of my students. I inwardly groan. I was one of the younger tenured professors, but still, the thought is bothersome.

"Reason you are staring, love?" His eyes crinkle before they shamelessly sweep over me, and I blush.

"How old are you?" I blurt.

"Not that it matters, but thirty-two. Plenty old enough to be drinking." He chuckles. "How old are you?"

"I… thought you were quite a bit younger than Gavin." I dodge the question. He has a year on me, and my assumptions proved embarrassing.

"It only seems that way. The old git never has aged well. I'm assuming you are about my age then?" He clearly is having quite a bit of fun as the humor never leaves his charismatic eyes.

"You've got a year on me. I could have sworn you were closer to my students' ages."

"Oh?"

"I teach college-level art."

"You thought I was some schoolboy swotting the books? You must be pissed already." His laugh booms out, deepening my blushing cheeks.

The bartender sets my drink down. I quickly chug it back, sheepishly looking away from my present company for a moment. I glance back to find his kind eyes on mine, leaning in much closer than before.

"Up for a game of pool?"

"Pool?"

"Yes."

"I've never really played much."

"Care to learn?" His wicked grin is quite enticing, not to mention the liquid courage now coursing through my veins, reminding me of a younger, cockier version of myself.

"Are you going to laugh at me when I make a fool of myself?" I counter with my own cheek.

"Probably." He sniggers as he rises to his full height from the stool, dwarfing me as he offers his hand.

"Barely know one another, and you are already drumming up plenty of dirt to poke fun at me with." I huff, scooting off the stool and into his hold.

"Not to worry, I will take extra special care." He winks. His soft brown hair carelessly falls forward, barely grazing his eyes.

My gaze lingers on his lovely face a bit too long as he speaks, causing his pupils to dilate and profile to darken in sudden hunger. Clearly, we are equally attracted to one another. Instead of validating my deep-seated feminine drive for such affections, it has the opposite effect. It makes me feel old, really old, and quite out of reach of such games played by young, attractive, and available people. As we edge to the back, we find all the tables full.

"Christ, looks like a bit of a wait. Can I get you another drink?" he offers as he places a few coins under the ledge of the closest table, holding our spot in line.

The first two had already worked me over and had me sitting at the edge of "properly buzzed" and "more will get you shit faced." Thank goodness I am wearing fitted jeans and not that mini skirt I contemplated. Just in case I plant it somewhere, at least I won't give the room full of young drinkers an eyeful. Go me for planning ahead. Perhaps I should wait a bit for another drink. I can't remember the last time I was drunk. That's a lie; I remember exactly the last time—a night out with my love, way before a life of cancer. The whirlwind of depression ebbs in the back of my mind, tempting to pull me under. I suck in a deep breath, and my mouth answers before I can be pulled under. "Sure."

He motions for me to wait next to the pool table and takes off back toward the bar. What the hell. When in Rome, right? It's not like I have to walk far to get a cab back to my hotel. Cabs are everywhere. If all these youngins can do it, I can certainly have one night of fun.

I'm not sure why I keep referring to all of these patrons as if I have decades on them. Most look to be in their late twenties or into their thirties, and I am far from grandmotherly. Or am I? Seems I have lost my way and no longer know how to have fun. How fucking depressing is that?

As I wait for James, an epiphany of sorts barrels through me like a shit ton of bricks. It's as if, for the first time, I've stepped outside of myself and had a third-party perspective view. All of James' jabs this evening, and my friends' jokes about my lack of ability to have fun, blows my mind. I used to be so free and fun loving, but now, the little hippy Jack fell in love with is long gone. Who am I?

"Whoa! Have you seen a ghost?" James' welcoming brown eyes come into view, zeroing me back into focus. Man, those are definitely the kind of eyes a girl could get lost in.

"Am I a dud?"

"What?" He rapidly blinks, trying to catch on.

"A dud, a bore, a snooze,"

"I almost forgot what strange names Americans come up with. I wouldn't go that far, but you certainly could do with a livening up." He winks at me.

"God, I don't even know how to anymore." I sigh, and my slender shoulders sag in a pathetic motion. Jack would be so pissed if he could see me now, the shell of the woman I once was.

"Here, start with this, and then I will give you a lesson in that," he offers as he nods to the pool table.

Sucking the straw into my mouth, I take a sip. The taste dances across my taste buds and dazzles me, finally lighting something that had long since flickered out. I boldly hold his gaze as I suck down the entire glass, chasing the unnamable, suddenly thirsty for life. Not sure what has overcome me in the moment, I go with it. The adventurous spur inspires something within his posture that I haven't noticed in a man in a long time. My heart hammers in my chest as the sudden sound of someone breaking the balls of a new game a few tables over makes me jump as James sways closer.

His lips brush my ear as he leans in. "Are you flirting with me?" His deep voice hums, lighting up my belly with fire.

My heartbeat picks up a notch as I realize what has happened. Popping the straw from my mouth, I turn and place my glass down on the bar in a sudden clinking of remaining ice. "Hey, look at that, our table is open!" I cheerfully sing and step away.

"Well then, let the lesson begin." Devious promises underline his words. This is definitely an experienced man who's played with a lot of ladies. Why am I not surprised? His defined forearms tick under his rolled-up sleeves as he chooses two cues from the rack before turning to me. "Now, this is called a 'cue,' and it is used for hitting those ball thingies," he jokes. The way he switches back and forth between humor and straight sex appeal will be the death of me, I am sure of it.

"Thanks for the remedial lesson. However will I make it through this game?" I feign like a southern damsel, adding a pout on the end for good measure. Sorcha would be proud; I learned that from her. I've never been an outwardly sexual being, but inspired by my desire to have fun with this character in front of me, I channel my best friend.

And that is how the night goes. We flirt back and forth as well as laugh. No one has made me laugh this hard and long in forever. Toward the end of our game, the "accidental" brushes of hand and grazing of hips become so frequent, I begin to wonder if he might pounce on me right here in the crowded pub. Feeling tipsy yet tired, and confused over how his presence has stimulated some long-suppressed female desires, I decide it's time to call it a night. It was nice to feel youthful and desired, even if just for a few hours.

"Hey, James, thanks for showing a girl how to have fun again. I am going to catch a cab." I smile, cheeks sore from the corners of my mouth being lifted high all night. The man has a great sense of humor.

"Let me see you out." He takes my hand, laces his fingers through mine, and leads the way.

My heart begins to pound in my ears, and the need to squeeze my thighs together at his touch threatens to sober me up. I haven't felt the intimate touch of a man since Jack. I never thought another man would inspire sexual need in my cold, dead loins again.

He leads me to the taxi stand but continues past just a ways. Confusion etches itself across my face as he turns to me. Tenderly running a hand up the back of my neck, he leans in to kiss me. My insides panic as turmoil races through my veins, threatening to choke the life out of me. The soft, plump flesh of his lips connects with mine, silencing my fears in one ridiculously hot kiss. He encourages me with his body, and, before long, my hands betray my head by running up his body as they hungrily pull him closer.

God help me, he smells so good. And this feels even better. To be touched, caressed, and desired. Heat and need bloom between us as the intensity builds. Hot hands suddenly grab my ass and pull me against his hard body, telling me just how far he is willing to go if I am game. Am I? Shit, my body is telling me hell yes! But the thought of sleeping with this prime piece of man is more than I can bear. No one has seen me naked since Jack, and I am not sure I can be that vulnerable with another man. Gently pulling away from our embrace, I smile once more at a lust-driven James, his eyes alight with deviant desires.

"Well, thank you for an amazing evening. But I am not so sure it is a good idea for you to come back with me to the hotel." I gaze at his lips, wondering what their caress would feel like all over my body.

"The way you are biting your lip and staring at me makes me think otherwise," he growls, taking my hand and pulling me into a cab I hadn't seen pull up. I collapse in the backseat, right into his side. We are scrunched together, his hand possessively clasping my inner thigh as he lounges back nonchalantly, even though his eyes keep drifting over my body. My insides are scrambling as I try to decide what I want. *Make up your mind, Jade.* He is willing, and I haven't had sex since long before Jack died. Thoughts of my lost husband cloud me and dampen my eyes out of nowhere. The thought of being with anyone else feels like the ultimate betrayal to his memory.

"Hey, Jade, you okay?" His fingers trace my cheek. He turns me to face him.

"Yeah, no… shit, I don't know. I haven't been with anyone else in a long time," I admit.

He leans in and pecks my cheek. "Not to worry, we don't have to do anything. I can just see you home, and then be on my way. But if you'll have me, I'd be honored." James's heartfelt gaze holds mine. The tenderness and concern there tells me everything I needed to know.

If nothing else, he is first and foremost a gentleman, and that alone makes my anxiety lax during a beat of vulnerability. We sit in silence, hypnotized by one another, as the cab inches closer to my looming hotel. My mind races as I seal my fate. I've never done "just sex," but I can manage it, right? People do it all the time. Judging by the way my body has flipped into overdrive, my loins are about ready to kick my brain in the metaphorical nuts and lock it up tight. The cab comes to halt in a subtle screech of brakes, severing our locked gaze, forcing me to blink. After I hop out, I look back to find him waiting, hand poised on the door.

"You coming?" I smile and keep walking. He quickly jumps out and jogs after me, looping a thick forearm around my waist and pulling me close, sending butterflies through me.

"I thought you'd never ask."

I curl back into bed and draw the comforter up around me, flipping open the screen on my laptop after I settle. Sorcha has been blowing up my phone, wanting to do a transatlantic catch up, so I call her.

Her face comes into view, freezing in between syllables of sound scratching across the connection. Finally, it clears, and vibrant eyes pin me hard.

"Who did you just fuck?"

I begin to sputter and look away, my cheeks burning.

"Don't you even try to pretend you didn't. Your lips are swollen, your hair is a mess, and I sure as hell know you don't wake up lookin' like that seeing as how you've woken up on my couch plenty." She snickers, a glimmer in her eye as her brash form of love comes through. She really is happy about this. I had been spiraling all morning about it. Well, after I saw James out.

"Yeah, your spidey senses are right."

She slaps something hard in the background. "It's about time! Who was it? Some exotic man you picked up in the bar?"

"Not exactly…" I trail off, knowing I can't lie to her.

"Well?"

"It was James." I sigh, fingers coming up to touch my bruised lips fondly in memory. Man, he was a good kisser.

"Really?" Sorcha's forehead crinkles as her eyes search me.

"It just kinda happened. He was a riot and quite the gentleman."

"Seems it runs in the family. Shit, not sure how Gavin is going to take this. He thinks of you like his little sister. And big ol' brother bear is super Dom and overbearing lately." She huffs and crosses her arms.

"Don't tell me that! I feel guilty enough about the whole mess. Maybe he doesn't need to know." My hands nervously tug at the sleeve of my robe.

"You really think I can keep it from him? And not get my ass paddled hard for it?" Her voice raises a few octaves.

"Sor, you are pregnant. He's not going to do it that hard." I snort. Her pregnancy hormones have her over-exaggerating everything. Then again, maybe not. I knew they liked to play hard, but I can't imagine him not being super careful. "By the way, how is he taking impending fatherhood?" She was so scared to tell him at first.

"I feel like I am trapped in a cage, and he only lets me out on a leash after he's thoroughly investigated all potential threats. I've barely just found out. I'm guessing I'm close to two months based on things, but I can't take seven more months of this!"

"Is it really that bad to have someone doting on you?" Heartbreak threatens me once more, the sense of grave loss never very far behind. Jesus, can't I get a break from that shit?

"Gah! Jade, I'm sorry. I didn't mean it like that. You know me, super independent and all. I tried to go down to the beach and photograph some tide pools the other day. Barely made it halfway down the path before he came barreling after me, stomping and making a stink about me going alone. It's the fucking beach! I've been down that little cliff path a hundred times."

"It's okay. I know ya didn't mean anything by it. Chill my friend, breathe, woo-saw. He's freaking out about becoming a dad, and he's just being overbearing as an outward reflection of his inner turmoil. Once the fear dies down, he'll loosen up."

"You sure about that?" Her voice is heavy with sarcasm.

"No, not entirely." I chuckle. Gavin was a control freak beforehand; I can't imagine now. "Seriously though, how does he feel about being a daddy?"

"It's hard to tell. He never wanted kids and made that quite clear from day one. I was cool with that. I was never sold on the notion either. He's wound tighter than a python around his dinner about the whole thing. But when we are curled up in bed, his fingers dance across my stomach, and I swear he was talking to my belly this morning when I woke up. We have our first appointment tomorrow; he went and called off work the whole damn day. The appointment is like what? Two hours tops?" She sighs in exasperation.

"At least he wants to be present and isn't running off to England to abandon you like your bestie did."

"Fucker knows I'd hunt his ass down if he ever tried some shit like that again. And you didn't abandon me; you are learning how to put that glow back into those cheeks…. Whatever you are doing, it's working." She winks at me, her green eyes shining bright as her auburn hair falls forward into her face. She is easily one of the most beautiful women I have ever met, inside and out, even if she is a bit too type-A and overly analytical at times.

"God, Sor, I feel so good and like the world's biggest asshole all at once," I blurt out of nowhere, on the verge on tears, the weight of my internal battle weighing thick again.

"Shhh, honey, why the hell would you say that? Whether you want to believe it or not, you are a single, beautiful, witty woman who is learning to live again. There is nothing wrong with that, so stop beating yourself up over it."

"I am trying. Logically, I get that, but my heart hurts so damn bad over it."

"Since when did the heart do anything but get us into trouble?" she jokes. I can't help but laugh. "Enough of the guilt shit. Ya gotta let that go. Now, more importantly, how was he in bed?"

"Oh my god, I am so not talking about that with you. Especially since you are shacked up with his brother."

"Inquiring minds want to know, how much *do* genetics play into sex abilities? I could run a study or something."

"Oh, hell no!" I bust out laughing before changing the subject because that is something she totally would do, out of nowhere, just for fun. She may be an artist, talented beyond belief with a camera, but that doctor in her is still alive and well despite her dropping that title like a ton of bricks.

Truth be told, the sex was amazing. James took his time with me in ways I've never experienced. It had been almost two years since a man touched me that way, and I am a bit afraid of what kind of beast he may have awoken. Squeezing my thighs together in memory, I do my best to focus on finishing this conversation with Sorcha. I've got to pack my bags and ready for the next leg of my trip.

Chapter 6

Jade

After a long day of traipsing around Old Town Square in Prague, I leave Tyn Church and head toward the quaint little Cafe Ebel that the locals at the breakfast place told me I had to try. I weave through the ancient walkways and scattered passersby. The scent of roasted coffee beans wafts down the corridor, drawing me in like a beacon. I round the bend and scurry up the cobblestone as a light breeze descends. The bell above the door announces my arrival into the antiquated shop as I take cover, anxious to wrap my hands around a hot mug and sit down after a long morning of wandering. Sure, most would be after lunch about this time, but the bread and cheese I packed had been enough.

The woman behind the register reminds me of my grandmother as she welcomes me with a warm smile, her chocolate eyes bringing me back to my childhood memories like a long-lost hug I didn't know I needed. After placing my order, I move down the counter to wait for my much-anticipated almond carrot cake and hot beverage. The little bell above the door alerts us to another's arrival, but I ignore it as I turn to search out the perfect table while the barista finishes steaming the milk. The sound of steam elicits a deep breath from me, lowering my shoulders. This leg of my journey has come quite a bit easier; it feels as if I am finally finding my stride. Thank goodness for that. Leaving London was hard but necessary, though

that first stop made me realize I had to begin the awakening I so
desperately needed.

"Jade?" A thick accent from distant memories makes my
heart speed up as I register the deep caress of his voice. I'd know it
anywhere. I turn in slow motion, my stunned gaze crashing into the
bluest eyes I've ever had the pleasure of being captured by.

"Shae?" It comes out more in a shocked grunt. I intended to
come across more confident than that, but the power of his presence
blew that out of the water.

"It's good to see ye, lass. What on earth are ye doin' on this
side of the world?" The corners of his mouth lift into a dazzling
smile, melting the world around us. What the hell is wrong with me?
I've gone from semi-confident, independent woman trekking the
world on her own to giddy schoolgirl within seconds of having my
old friend's attention once again turned upon me.

"I…" My voice travels off as he shamelessly rakes his eyes
down my body, taking me in like a starved man before returning
them back to my face, on his best behavior. "…needed to get away
from it all and see the world." My attention quickly shifts to the man
behind the counter handing over my goodies. Accepting them in
gratitude, I hold onto them for dear life as I try to figure out where to
go next.

Do I simply say 'see you later' like a stunned idiot or invite
him to sit? I haven't seen or heard from him in a year, not since the
water-lantern ceremony. My heart seizes with emotion as it all comes

flooding back, candid coffee breaks, him seeing me at my worst, the lanterns being taken out to sea—all stirred by the handsome lines of his face. My hand begins to shake, the fork clattering against the cakes plate as coffee begins to slosh over the side. Shae's grin presses into a firm line as he promptly takes my cup and plate from me.

"Come on then; we have a lot of catchin' up to do." He takes control and leads the way over to a little bistro table. Daftly, I follow, at a loss for words, my mind scrambling. Moments ago, I was mulling over the ancient stained glass windows of the last church I visited before coming here, and now ghosts from a year ago are swarming my head.

Once seated, he places my items on the table, gives me an odd look, and then turns to get his own. It doesn't take long before he sits before me, assessing me with those eyes that see straight through to my soul, continuing to render me speechless as I contemplate the probability of actually running into him out of the blue, halfway across the world in this little ancient city. Gone was the brotherly type energy he used to emanate, or did I just make that all up back when I couldn't conceptualize anything beyond the tragedy at hand? Had this always been there?

"How have you been?" His eyes light up as they narrow in on my mismatched ones. He seems to be anxiously attempting to read every possible emotion and experience mapped across the lines now formed there.

"I don't even know where to start. I haven't heard a peep out of you since that day on the beach." Perhaps it would have been better to begin with pleasantries, but some damaged part of me demanded I jump to the heart of the matter.

His face falls momentarily before picking back up. "I tried to pick up the phone, and wrote a dozen emails before deletin' them all." Shae's looks at the café's windows, unnamed emotions flitting over him.

"Why didn't you?" Pain laces my words, a hurt I hadn't realized even existed there. I told myself a hundred times he was simply an angel of the moment, providing me with a bit of solace so that my mind didn't completely up and walk out. A shoulder to lean on when I was on the verge of snapping under the weight of the pain.

"Because words failed me," he deadpans, his eyes finding mine once more as his broad shoulders sag.

"Failed you?" Disbelief clouds me as I grapple with the rush of foreign emotions. Why did this bother me so much?

"Well, this is a wee bit awkward of a reunion, straight to the point with ye." He clears his throat and sips his drink. A distant portion of my thoughts begins to long for London, scolding me for leaving prematurely. James was a tad hurt with my departure, but the fun he offered had me running scared. But in the face of the current shifts in reality I now sense taking place, that no-strings fun sounds good about now.

"It's fine, Shae, really. God…" I shake my head and pick up my fork, digging into the soft, decadent cake with gusto, wanting this moment I have periodically questioned the possibility of manifesting to simply end.

"I've missed ye," he breathes.

"Missed me? You barely knew me." I huff and palm up the steaming mug, my sass streaming through as my eyes skeptically track his every move.

"Really? Ye are going to quickly dismiss the validity of our brief yet intense time together?" Now it is his turn to attempt to mask some darting discomfort.

"It was what it was, a lovely, friendly distraction at a horrific time. What did you say at the time? You were just 'paying it forward.'" God, what is wrong with me? This is not how reunions should go, and where has all this bitterness come from?

"Are ye sayin' ye've missed me, too?" A spark returns to his dazzling eyes, his handsome face lighting up, and not put off by my snark at all.

My stern face softens. "I suppose I have." I really have—not that I want to admit that.

"I've missed ye as well, more than ye know."

"Then why the radio silence?"

"What do ye say to a woman who's captured yer heart, but is grievin' the loss of her husband?" And there it is. Vomit rises in the back of my throat as my stomach sinks. I hadn't thought about that. The weight of his truth threatens to drown me as I internally collect myself.

"Hi? How are you? Pleasantries are usually a nice start," I mumble as I attempt to chase away thoughts of my Jack, and the plaguing guilt I've been carrying since my London indiscretion.

He does a little eye roll to that and sips from his cup. Two shots of espresso, straight up, not much has changed. I smile to myself.

"What?" He looks about as if he spilled something.

"Still no frills with the coffee, I see."

"No point in ruinin' a perfectly good cup with all that." He lifts his chin toward my drink of choice, the mood finally lifting with some friendly banter.

"I prefer to call it an enhancement, kinda like social realism for the people's movement." I grin, baiting him into a deep conversation on art politics, something I have missed, and that proves to be easy, neutral ground for us.

Not many have been able to hold their own with me on a topic I feel so deeply about, but this man has always given me a run. He takes a deep breath and eases back into his seat, a glimmer back in his eyes as our reciprocated unease shifts into familiar ground. The minute he opens his mouth, my shoulders relax as joy overtakes me, easing us into a philosophical conversation. It's nurturing for our wayward souls. We need stimulation on the intellectual degree. Simple dinners and comradery has been nice, but to have my mind stirred on this level is sublime. God, I've wanted this. The minutes slip into hours as the sun begins to set, and we haven't stopped talking. Our discussion moves into his travels and projects while only lightly touching on how I have been. I wasn't ready to delve into that, and he seemed to understand my hesitation. After he wraps up how he ended up in Prague to restore an old historical home for a wealthy family, I hear my stomach growl and glance out the quaint windows to see orange streaking into dark blues across the sky.

"Ye need to eat. Let's head up the road to grab a bite." It wasn't a question, and I don't know whether to be flattered or taken aback by that.

"Well then, someone's being a bit bossy," I tease, trying to sidestep this new dominate side of him that did things to me I wasn't ready for.

"You have no idea." He winks. Gone is the boyish friend, quickly replaced by that hungry man who devoured me with a single look hours ago. "Now, the only choice I will be giving ye is if ye'd like to freshen up before dinner or head straight there."

"You're going to force me to come to dinner with you whether I want to or not?" I incredulously ask, my cheeks blazing under the heat of his stare, the intimacy of the moment becoming threatening.

"Quite simple, really. Ye ain't gettin rid of me that easily, not after all this time." He stands and clears our dishes off to the busing station as I grapple with my emotions.

Part of me wants to leap at every possible second to be at his side, and the other broken bits cry in fear, telling me to run the other way. *It's just dinner, Jade, it's not like you have to sleep with him if you don't want to.* But what if I do want to? What kind of person does that make me? A whore? What have I become?

Shae comes to stand by me, expectantly waiting.

Nerves threaten my legs as I stand, but I make the decision on the way up. "I'd like to freshen up first."

"Wonderful, where are you staying?"

"Art Deco Imperial."

"Naturally. I'll see ye to it then." His face breaks into a heart-stopping smile as he leads the way.

The taxi stops in front of the gorgeous hotel I couldn't pass up when looking for a place online to book, and Shae promptly jumps out to open my door. I pop out of the cab, fueled by nerves. He closes the door behind me and moves to take my arm, but I stop in my tracks.

"You don't have to walk me to the door. I can meet you there." My heart thuds in my chest. The thought of him anywhere near my hotel room is enough to make me feel lightheaded. We are simply old friends reuniting after a long absence. There's no need to jump ahead of ourselves.

"Yes, I do. And I happen to be stayin' here as well." He tugs me forward. My feet happily follow as my mind lags in hesitancy.

"Really? What's with all these coincidences?" My voice jumps an octave.

"My lovely Jade, I don't believe in coincidences." His large hand reaches forward, opening the front door to the hotel, leading me through with pride.

"Shae, this is absurd. Did Gavin somehow put you up to this?" My mind reels, the analytical side kicking into overdrive as we head through the little lobby toward the elevator.

"Gavin? How would he have anythin' to do with us endin' up in the same place at the same time, lass? I haven't spoken to him since I last saw ye." His quizzical eyes search mine as we wait for the elevator. A rebuttal plays on my lips, but I'm captured momentarily by their depths. The bell announcing the arrival of the lift has me stuttering. The corner of his mouth turns up as he once again pulls me forward, my feet dragging between two worlds, past and present.

"Jade?" His voice reaches through to me with a hint of humor.

"What?" I shake my head, quickly looking away for fear of getting lost again for eternity in my dear friend's eyes. I've got to get it together.

"What floor?" His long fingers hover over the buttons as the door chimes closed.

"Three, please." It's all I can do not to stutter out the damn words.

"Excellent. I'm just above you then." He makes quick work of buttons while I stare off into space. As much as I try to ignore his looming presence by my side, it's hard not to feel his eyes on me, which makes my cheeks betray me. The bell chimes, and the door opens to my floor. I quickly rush off without giving him a second glance. Digging in my bag for the room key in a hurry, I get to my door and fumble about, my unease making the simple task impossible. After a few misguided attempts, success is reached as a deep voice noisily clears his throat next to me. It causes my body to jump, and a squeak escapes my throat.

"Shae! You scared the crap out of me!" I smack his arm, the hard contour of his bicep stinging my hand.

"Ye jumped off so damn fast that we never set a time for dinner."

"I'm not getting out of this, am I?"

"Not on yer life." His cheek dimples, nearly stopping my heart in its tracks. I scold myself internally and shake my head once more.

"Fine. Give me thirty?"

"Very well." He gives a small bow before sauntering off to the lift with a loose-hipped swagger that sends the perpetual butterflies living my stomach into a frenzy.

Has he always had a stride like that? And an ass that looks that good in slacks? Not wanting to give it any more thought, I swing my door open and run to my closet in a panic. What do I wear? My hands run through the few long, linen skirts I brought, but nothing seems right. Dinner—this is a dinner date. Sure, just with a friend, but I certainly don't want to be seen as the homely American at his side. Jeez, just sitting in the coffee shop, I felt inadequately dressed in his presence. The man knew how to fill out some fine threads. I contemplate calling Sorcha and waking her pregnant ass up, but I ditch the idea as I spy the tight black dress she insisted on throwing in my suitcase 'just in case I met someone worth impressing' on my travels.

My mind races through all the possible scenarios should I venture down the path of this so-called, 'friendly dinner.' I'm not an idiot, well, perhaps a little bit. I keep telling myself we are just friends, even though he kept looking at me all day as more than that. *Chuck it in the fuck-it bucket* as Samuel likes to say. Grabbing the dress and a pair of heels, I get dressed as fast as possible and skitter into the bathroom to freshen my makeup. As the brush sweeps across my lid to finish my smoky eye, a knock sounds out from the door. Steeling my nerves, I raise my eyes to the ceiling and send a silent prayer to whoever may be listening as I slowly snap my eyeshadow closed and toss everything back into the bag.

"Coming." I stop by the desk mirror by the door to smooth the lines of my dress. It has a halter strap and small slit up the back, and I make sure everything is covered. Doing a little turn and fluffing my wavy hair, I blow out through pursed lips as I open the door. My breath catches at the sight before me.

There is Shae, looking quite debonair in fitted, black dress pants and a pressed silk button-up in a shade of azure blue. It matches his eyes perfectly. His ginger hair is now parted and slicked, adding to the polished effect. My words get lost in my throat.

"Well then, glad I went with a dress shirt or I wouldn't have been fit to be at yer side. Ye look lovely. Stunnin' actually." In a nervous fashion, his fingers tug at his collar, the years falling off his mature face to that of a younger man.

"Thank you." My chin drops, and I look up at him through my lashes. I had just begun to get used to his newer, cockier side, and now a peek into his vulnerability made this all the more difficult. I don't want to feel anything for him but the reinvigorated, comfortable friendship we founded a year ago. Something now tells me it's not going to be that simple, and that scares the crap out of me.

"Ready to go?" I change my tune to a peppier one, ready to get this over with. In and out, it's only one meal. Then I can get back to my travels, plan the next leg of my journey to Brussels for a taste of beer, chocolate, and Art Nouveau before dropping down to Paris for the almighty Louvre. I can taste the cultural variances now, food and art satiating my starved palate at each stop. With each day, this adventure has gotten easier, and I find myself looking forward to things instead of feeling the heaviness of loneliness.

"After ye." He extends his arm toward the elevator.

I palm up my clutch and room key from the desk and march forward, a woman on a mission.

Halfway down the hall, a strong hand comes around and slows my pace.

"Are ye gonna wait for me?" he chides as he loops my arm through his, instantly bringing me into his personal space and halting my hurried stance.

"Sorry," is all I can manage as I avoid eye contact.

"Is everythin' all right?" He extends a finger and guides my eyes toward his by way of lifting my chin.

"Yeah, just hungry and ready to get there." Well, it is part of the truth. His stern jaw flexes as he looks right through me. His nostrils flare, but he lets it go as he escorts me to the lift. It takes me until the hotel lobby to find the courage to speak. Who knows why my nerves have strangled my common decency. Perhaps it was the close proximity of the mechanical box assisting our descent toward food… or the fact that he somehow felt bigger standing next to me than I remembered.

"So, Shae, where ya takin' me?" I attempt with a smile as we finally get close to the door.

"It's a surprise." His deepening voice rumbles through me, causing my already-anxious heart to jump another notch, nearing combustion.

"Oh." My eyes search his as he leads on toward the taxi stand. One is conveniently awaiting our arrival, and he ushers us straight in. I gaze out the window as he gives the address. He settles into the backseat next to me, his knee brushing my bare one, sending an electrical impulse up my thigh and straight to a place that not even James managed to awaken. A place I long thought to be dead, much like my cold and distant heart. I must have made a sound because his hand suddenly lifts and wraps around mine, bringing it to rest on his knee.

"It's a beautiful evenin'. Even all the stars came out for us." He tries to ease my tension, running his thumb over my palm.

My breathing picks up, the intimacy of it all too much for this downtrodden woman. How did we go from heated political conversations laden with banter and sarcasm to this in a course of one random day? I'm on the verge of telling the taxi to take me back to my hotel when we come to a stop outside of the cutest wine bar I have ever seen. The smells of fresh baked bread and smoked meats float in through the open window, baiting me into continuing while my head is screaming an escape plan.

Shae hops out and comes around to open my door, so that I don't have to scoot across in my short dress. Within minutes, Shae is leading me up to the host like a proud peacock, many heads turning our way in this quaint little setting. There are only about a dozen tables, an open bar with seats, and it is packed. I should have stuck with my hippy skirt instead of this dress. I inwardly groan, cheeks flushing under the pressure of strange eyes.

"Ye need to stop tryin' to hide yer beautiful face behind that hair. They're only lookin' because not even the sun can hold up against yer radiance." His hand takes mine, bringing it up to brush his lips against my flesh.

My knees damn near buckle as my body is set aflame. Nope, friends don't do that to one another. Frozen on the spot, I become a deer in the headlights, the host's beckoning voice in the background fuzzing in and out as my eyes lock on his. What the hell is going on between us? Completely pleased with himself, he smiles and turns to escort me to the table that is ready for us. A table set for two, candlelight… all set in this tiny little wine bar, with a modernized interior set within an ancient-looking building, in the middle of freaking Prague. My mouth guppies a bit as he pulls out my chair, and I deftly sit down, trying to get it together. My body does nothing but be disloyal to me left and right around this man, who is supposed to just be a friend. No one has ever had this effect on me, and why the fuck did it have to start now? I'd rather not convert into a fumbling, teenage girl at the moment. Shae orders two wine-tasting sets along with something I don't catch before I am able to get my flight reflexes under control and not bolt from the restaurant.

"What do ye think?" he eagerly asks, his hands making quick work to place his napkin over his lap.

"It's nice." My voice cracks like a prepubescent boy's as a waiter descends, filling our water glasses and asking if we would like to order. How attractive I must be now.

"We will start with the smoked salmon and quiche of the day please," Shae smoothly replies. I hadn't even had time to look at the menu. Then again, I haven't looked anywhere else but at him.

After the waiter walks away, Shae asks, "Jade, we haven't seen each other in a year. Why are ye clammin' up on me?" The intensity he emits rises, his chin coming to rest atop his clasped hands.

"I don't know." It comes out automatically, and he snorts in reply.

"Now ye've taken to lyin'?" He calls my bluff instantly.

"Can't we discuss the importance of the Dada movement or even argue who pioneered 19th century modernization propagandistic art?" I shift forward and grasp my water, my throat tight.

"Does yer brain ever want a break? Or does it never cease?"

The waiter comes back and sets our wine-tasting racks with the mini glasses in front of us while kindly explaining to us which is which, although I am struggling to pay attention. It is too hard with those amazing blue eyes making me feel things I don't want to feel.

After the waiter departs, I upend one of the Italian reds without a second thought. The dryness constricts my throat, so I chase it with a swig of ice-cold water, quite unladylike in an establishment like this.

"Yer supposed so savor, roll it across yer palate." He picks up a glass, scents it deeply before slowly sipping it, his tongue chasing the departing glass to catch an escaping drip as he grunts in approval. Even his grunt has a Scottish appeal. That has to be one of the sexiest things I have ever seen. I am so messed up in the head. *He's just a friend. He's just a friend*, I remind myself.

"Very well." I pick up another glass, thoughtfully doing as he suggests with a rosier red. The fruit undertones are delicious. Under the heat of his unnerving, burning stare, I sip again and moan in delight before upending the glass once more, the need for liquid courage suddenly greater than my desire to enjoy fermented grapes.

"I take it ye like that one?" His voice deepens as he continues seductively sampling his own, torturing me without even knowing it.

I move to the third taster, and make quick work of it, the scent of his cologne driving me mad from across the table. Thanks to being a lightweight who hasn't eaten a proper meal since breakfast, the wine hits me. The tension starts to dissipate as our food is brought out in tapas fashion, perfect for two to share, naturally. And to think, he was able to get us a table here in such a short amount of time. The smoked salmon hits my senses, and I eagerly dive in without another thought, my hunger getting the best of me. He smirks to himself as he follows suit.

As the food hits my system, and my shaking quells, I am able to tune more into my environment. The sounds of fellow diners digging in deep to their experience provides an ambient backdrop as laughter, chatter, and hushed exchanges bloom all about. The sounds of the kitchen sneak out from under a semi-closed door while the barkeeps work hard at popping wine corks and filling orders. Such a perfect little place; he really does know me well.

"Penny for yer thoughts?" Shae attempts to bait me into casual talk.

"I was just taking in this place. It's quite perfect. How did you get us a spot so fast?" This seems to please him as he seduces me with that damn dimple before slating some quiche over to his plate.

"The owner is the one who hired me. Now that ye are calmer, care to share why ye've been actin' like a tree'd cat?"

"Things feel more than friendly all of a sudden. I wasn't prepared for that."

"Oh?"

"Or is it just me feeling things that are way beyond the friend zone?" Enter liquid courage. I am on a mission with this trip. Who has time for beating around the bush?

"No, it certainly isn't just ye." He levels his gaze, ready to meet me head-on. God, I love how he's not afraid to honestly go head to head with me on any topic. I know I can be a bit of a handful once my spirit is stirred by something. Even my beloved husband would fall quiet at times, happier to let me rant and get it out of my system than engage.

"Why the change?"

"Nothin's changed." He shrugs and picks up his last tasting glass.

"Come again?" For some reason, his omission spikes my fury. I slam my last sample and motion for our waiter.

"Why do ye think I failed to contact ye?"

I order another glass from our attractive waiter, who looks me over one last time before taking off to fill my request, buying me a moment.

"Who knows… you were busy?" Enter my sass on liquid courage.

"It's not like ye to play dumb, and we both know ye to be far from it."

"What do you want me to say?"

"The truth as it sits."

"The truth is I have no clue."

"Very well. I felt like a real ass contactin' the woman I fell for as she was grievin' her husband."

"Fell for? Me? We barely spent any time together," I state incredulously, downing a piece of quiche, trying to keep my mouth from flying off any more.

"Time enough to know I couldn't deny my attraction to your brilliant, slightly mad mind." He offsets his minutely wounded pride with a comment he knew would make me blush and cut straight to my heart.

"And here I thought you were just a glutton for punishment."

He shakes his head. "Glutton, perhaps."

"And here we sit."

"That we do." His eyes momentarily eat me alive before settling back into his relaxed state.

Doubts of having a handle on his intentions fly out the door as I internally level with myself. It's been less than twenty-four hours, shit, less than twelve, and I already find myself dreading his departure at the end of the night. My heart might not be available for any one ever again, but what is the harm in enjoying this evening with an old friend?

"So this is a real date?" I know I sound like an idiot.

"That it is." He studies me, trying to read where this is going, grappling with his own emotions as his handsome face captures my attention.

Heat rushes to my chest and neck as the wine flushes me, along with the validation of this dinner date.

My glass of wine arrives along with another round of finger foods Shae insisted on when I ordered a refill. Looking at the glass, and then at him, I realize I am not hungry for food any more. But it would be a shame to waste all of this. Giving in to his request for lighter conversation, I regale him with my tales of adventures through London and Prague as we pick over the tapas and sip our wine. Time does what it always does when we are together. and I stop resisting what comes naturally between us. It isn't until we see someone sweeping up that we realize we are the last ones here, and our lovely hosts are trying not to be rude.

"Guess we better get on then." Shae quickly pays the bill. He ushers us out to the taxi stand, ever the gentleman.

Before I know it, we enter a time warp that brings us to standing outside of my hotel room, holding hands, saying lingering goodbyes.

"Goodnight, sweet Jade. Thank ye for joinin' me." His hand comes up to lightly brush my cheek as he leans in, wanting to kiss me, but holding back. The heat radiating from him coalesces with the drink we had, drugging us into a haze.

"Goodnight, Shae." Neither of us move, heavenly forces beyond our control cementing us. Electricity sparks in the air as his fingertips travel down the column of my neck, a magnetic pull I am tired of resisting. He feels entirely too good for this to be wrong. "Shae?" I whisper, partially praying he doesn't hear me, as I am unsure who's in control at the moment.

"Hmmm?" he manages through his transfixed state.

"Kiss me?" Why the fuck did I just say that? Internally, I scream at myself, questioning my boldness.

My heart pounds, rattling my chest, as I suck in a breath, waiting on edge for a response. He goes blank for a second before locking onto me, a starved man, ready for his first meal in ages. Frozen, I don't know what to expect, a crushing force like with James? A sweet surrender like my lost love? It's not like I have much experience to go by. His gaze cuts through me, triggering my mind to spiral into dangerous thoughts of self-loathing. As if reading my unease, he gently leans in and claims my mouth in a searing kiss. The connection is so hot it fries my brain on impact.

He is gentle yet forceful, coming at me like a freight train, giving me nowhere to hide. Running his tongue over my lips, he seeks entrance. I part for him with a gasp wrought with overwhelming emotions. He growls deep in his chest as he penetrates my mouth, owning it, as his hands come to rest on either side of my head against the door he has me pressed into. My body melds to his, happy for the intimate closeness of another. It's terrible of me to compare, but nothing about my experience with James was very intimate. It was mechanical, but fun.

Suddenly feeling self-conscious about our public display in a lighted hallway, I breathlessly pull away, his lips chasing mine fleetingly before he realizes my discomfort and backs up a bit.

"What is it? Ye okay?" He runs his thumb over my bottom lip as the elevator chimes down the hall, and another couple steps out, grinning as they see us. My head turns the opposite way into his propped up arm to hide my face. His hand drops from caressing my cheek and sneaks the room key out of my hand, promptly opening the door. Snaking an arm around my waist, he backs me into the room, shutting us away from prying eyes.

"Is that better?" He lifts my chin so that I once again cannot hide.

"Yes," I breathe before biting my trembling lower lip.

His soft mouth lowers to mine at a more sedate pace. It starts deliberate and cautious, but as my body becomes like a live wire, hungrily meeting him head-on, we quickly achieve our previous stride. Firm hands grip my hips, forcing me closer as they travel toward the zipper on my back. Cool air kisses my freshly exposed skin, and I shiver in delight, pressing my breasts into his firm chest. The warm pads of his fingers begin to lightly explore my back as they travel up and around to slip the offending article from my shoulders. As it falls away, our kiss deepens, and my hands tear at his shirt. Buttons fly to meet the ground in a little clink of plastic on hardwood as my palms smooth across his chiseled physique. He breaks our kiss to shuck off his shirt, his lips red and puffy. His brilliant blue eyes find mine, waiting for permission to continue. His constant consideration for me is quite endearing and extremely validating for my womanhood.

Reaching around, I unhook my bra, letting it fall before instinctively covering myself with my hands.

"Don't hide from me," Shae reprimands, his voice deepening in a governing way, sending heat straight to my pussy.

My hands fall away, baring myself before his approving stare. He can't take his eyes from my body as he makes quick work of the rest of his clothes, the two of us now visually exploring one another. His body is ridiculous. I hadn't realized how in shape he is. Oh my god, and he has intricate tattoos sleeve on his arms, telling a story which I do not know. Images dance with Polynesian-inspired lines, all inked within his skin. You'd never know in his normally pressed business attire that he was tatted to this degree. It is so hot. I don't have any tattoos, and neither did my fallen angel. Everything about this man in front of me is different, and far from anything I have experienced. He is exquisite, and he wants me. Forgetting all about my own embarrassment of having a stranger see me naked, I give into the riptide and fold forward into his waiting arms, wanting nothing more than to have them around me, to finally be lost in the embrace of another.

Skin on skin, fire ignites. As if sensing the crumbling of my resolve to fight whatever exists between us, Shae picks up the pace, eagerly backing me deeper into the room, roaming my body with his desperate hands, setting it aflame. I'm pressed against him, our mouths battling for more and more. His erection digs into my abdomen, causing my hips to undulate all on their own. A throaty groan escapes him as he eases me back onto the bed and glides down to settle between my legs. The motion was smooth, effortless, perfectly executed, and has me panting hard. He feels amazing. Who am I kidding? Finally being this close, this intimate, with someone I feel close to is miraculous. His mouth kisses down my inner thigh, alerting me to his next intention, which kind of freaks me out. Feeling me tense, he stops.

"Jade?" His thick accent rolls across my flesh, making the inner conflict now taking place worse.

"Sorry, I've never had that done before," I sheepishly admit. It wasn't like I've never had an offer; it was more of a personal thing. It felt selfish to me to expect that of a man. The heart of the matter is, in sex, the man does much of the work, trying to get us in the mood and keep us there. Asking for that on top of all the other pleasure seems selfish in my book. I know others enjoy giving and receiving in that department. Personally, I liked to give. I didn't need to receive.

"Never?" His brow hits the ceiling. I shake my head and bite my lip. "Lie back—"

I cut him off. "Shae, really, it's okay. I don't need that—" He doesn't let me finish.

"But I do. I love it. Now, lie back… Please?" His tone is softer, considerate, but remains edged with stoutness.

Hesitantly, I comply, but only as far as leaning back on my elbows as he settles down with purpose, his eyes never leaving mine.

Using his nose to part my lower lips, he inhales deeply and groans. "Aye, yer honey is sweeter than any rose."

It is an act that equally turns me on and makes me self-conscious. Did he just really do that? I feel a bit disgusted by my intrigue, and invigorated all in one. As my thoughts spiral, one heavy hand comes to rest on top of my lower stomach as the other sneaks between my legs. My hips squirm as my unfamiliarity with what is about to happen gets the best of me, but I don't get far. That gentle caress soon turns firm, immobilizing my fidgety form. As much as I want to protest, curiosity gets the better of me. Our gazes are locked. His pink tongue jets out with perfect aim and strikes my clit in an intimate caress. Electricity shoots down my thighs on contact, and a small moan, unbeknownst to me, escapes my throat. *What the hell*? I think to myself as I bask in the sensations now descending.

With small flicks of his tongue, he delights in tasting me, the pleasure obvious in his passion-filled baby blues. Hungrily, he dives in, sucking, licking, and dragging his tongue throughout every inch of my pussy. White-hot flames consume every bit of my hyperexcited flesh, and my legs tremble as he savors me like the world's finest dessert. It is the hottest fucking thing I have ever experienced. Fisting my hair with one hand, the other barely holding me up, I jump when I feel a finger stroke my entrance before slipping in and languidly circling, hovering just inside.

"Oh, fuck," I scream as my hands drop to clench the bedding and my head falls back, unable to focus. The added pressure has me climbing at record speed to the peak of orgasm, tortuously hovering there, desperate for some form of greater penetration. The need to be filled more thoroughly in order to get my release claws at the flesh of my ass in an ache as my hips shift, trying to get those thick, strong fingers to go deeper. Shae growls; the reverberation has me crying out in frustration. A second finger joins the first. Together, they travel deeper inside of me, giving me more of what I need. So close, fuck, I am so close. I begin to pant as my body shakes in need.

"Mhm," he moans as he sucks on my clit, pulling it between his lips, grazing it lightly with his teeth as he vigorously finger fucks me. The vibration of his masculine tone against my flesh adds to everything else, tipping me over the edge. Lights flash in front of my eyes as a multifaceted, enormous orgasm rips through me.

"Shae!" I scream his name as he slowly continues to work me, not allowing me to come down. Instead, he sends me over into another immediate release. I pant and cry his name over and over as I ride the pulsating waves of pleasure, happily lost, blissed into a complete state of not giving a shit if I ever come back down. Slowly groaning and rocking his hands, he slows his motions and finally tears his mouth from feasting on me. His eyes latch onto my glassed-over ones as he prowls up my body. The muscles in his shoulders and biceps bunch as he goes, the azure blue of his ravenous gaze calling to me as he licks his swollen lips.

"Thank ye, beauty, the pleasure was all mine." He claims my mouth, my spice saturating the kiss, adding a new erotic thrill I'd never even thought I'd like.

The thick head of his cock pushes at my apex. My legs naturally fall apart before coming up to wrap around Shae's waist, my body's hungry for more. I need him so much closer. I need to feel him deep inside of me. Fuck, I need this so bad.

"Not yet. I need to relish in you more." Shae leans back to grin before lowering his head to draw my taut nipple into his mouth.

My back arches off the bed as need drives me into a crazed state, the previous orgasms doing nothing to lessen it. It's been a long time since I've been this vulnerable and intimate with someone, and he's opened me like a book in no time. Shae is ecstasy defined, and my broken, lonely heart wants to drown in his warm, encompassing depths.

"Shae, please, please take me," I beg without realizing, lost in the surrender.

He slows his laving of my heavy breasts and trails kisses across my collarbone before coming to rest his forehead on mine. Shifting his hips, he painstakingly eases the head of his erection into my core, and then stops, making me cry in frustration.

"Easy, lass. This is our first time. I want to revel in every moment with ye. I have fantasized about this since the moment I laid eyes on ye."

His admission strikes my frozen heart, cracking a fissure into the cold exterior. I stare into his fathomless blue depths and get lost; the connection centers me back into the emotional intensity of the moment instead of letting my body's needs take over and drive. It's easy to separate the two. It would be far too easy to let our bodies go to town in an emotionless state, which is how it went with James. But not Shae; he won't allow that. And, after what we've shared, how can I deny him by not being fully present in this moment?

Somehow, wrapped in his arms, it doesn't seem as scary as I might have thought. Inch by inch, he takes his time feeding himself into me, the sensations more profound, as well as agonizing at this pace. As he pushes in to the hilt, pleasure rips from my chest. He stills, filling me completely, allowing me a moment to adjust to his size as he pulsates inside, making me quiver and shake while he kisses and nips at my neck. Gently, he pulls back until the head is barely contained, the absence like a void. I yelp in frustration again, wanting every inch of his beautiful dick stretching me. Answering my call, he slams back into my wetness, gliding all the way in with force, changing my cries of frustration into those of raw, unadulterated pleasure. As he begins to drive into me over and over, his masculine scent and powerful presence trigger me to transcend the physical binds of my body on a wave of pleasure overload. Each stroke of his cock colors me his, his driving flesh imprinting new life into my very soul. For the first time in forever, I feel completely alive in this heady state. Together, our bodies coalesce in a wondrous symphony as we reach the apex. His breath pistons in and out of his chest, the muscles in his torso flex and bunch, rippling his beautiful ink as he takes us to the edge.

"Come with me, my beauty," Shae growls, his deep, Scottish accent rocketing through me, forcing my body to comply. The headboard provides a deafening boom as it slams into the wall with his final thrust, and we come undone, together, screaming each other's names. The world stops; nothing exists outside of our connection as we ride it out. As one last shiver rockets through our bodies, his heavy form collapses atop me and my legs fall splayed, both of us spent to the max, neither of us able to move aside from our attempt to recover our collective breathing.

"Fuck, y'er stunnin'," he rasps while placing a feather-light kiss on my cheek. "Y'er eyes… one blue, one green, like God tried to paint ye with perfection because one color just wouldn't do for his rare masterpiece."

His words fall softly around me, the pillow talk sweet, threatening to crack that hairline fissure he's already managed to make wide open, exposing the bits I never want anyone to see or touch within me, parts meant only for Jack. On defensive instinct, I begin to shut back down, detaching emotionally from our profound experience.

Shae eases out of me, rolling onto his side. This absence is worse than the pain and guilt now eating away at my center. Sitting up on one elbow, he dances his fingers through the ends of my long, wavy hair.

"Ye all right, lass?" The tone of his voice in on edge, seeking validation of my wellbeing.

"Ya, sorry, just trying to take it all in." Internally, I scramble. That was easily the best sex I'd ever had, and I hate myself for it. It all feels like one giant betrayal.

"Did I hurt ye?" Stress tightens his features, and I can tell the thought of the possibility pains him. God, I can't let him sit with that.

Turning into him, I tenderly brush back his disheveled, copper hair. "Lord no, not in the least! That was the best I ever had, Shae. Thank you." I have to give him something, as much as it feels like a knife to the heart to share or admit anything that might damage or taint my memories of Jack. The glorious man next to me deserves a sliver of the truth after gifting me with this memorable night I will treasure forever.

He releases the breath he was holding, the stress lines smoothing from his face. "Phew! Ye had me worried for a minute. I got carried away, prayed I didn't go too far."

"Not at all, promise. It was…" I trail off, my voice hoarse.

"Unreal. Never knew it could feel like that," Shae finishes for me.

"Like what?"

"Like yer on drugs but not."

"Yeah, I guess it did feel a lot like that." I smile.

"Do ye want me to stay the night?"

Darkness returns to the forefront of my mind. I've already made up my mind that I am booking it to Belgium first thing tomorrow. Any more time with him, and I risk losing myself completely. Would being wrapped up in his warmth a few more hours be so bad? I hadn't realized how much I have been craving physical contact with another until him. It's a long needed salve, and it's all I can do to keep my resolve and not completely come undone in his presence.

"Yeah, that'd be nice." I reach up to kiss the tip of his nose before nestling into him.

He drops to his back, slides his hands around my waist, and brings me along so I am now sprawled over the top of him, my cheek coming to lie on his pec. "Rest that mind of yours now."

The deep *lub-dub* of his beating heart lulls me under; the security of his arms allowing me to let go. No matter what happens, he's got me, which brings a sense of peace that not even my friends could give.

Chapter 7

<u>Shae</u>

The muffled sound of Jade's restful breathing echoes through the still night air. Regretfully, I shift her to my side as our shared body heat is proving to be a bit much at the moment. She stirs and adjusts before settling right back into me, as if she cannot get close enough. Lord in heaven, how did this come to be? I never thought myself to be a bad person per se, but worthy of this? What on earth did I do to get so incredibly lucky? Her presence has haunted me over the last year, almost to a painful degree. I attempted and failed to date here and there, but no one ever compared. Even playing a tad at my local kink club held no interest.

To be honest, that's how I knew Gavin prior to our actual meeting on that horrid day. Blood and panic floods my memory as I recall seeing her walk into oncoming traffic, horns blaring, and her clothes covered in blood. Worst of all, the expression on her face was one that will follow me to the grave. Complete shock, pain, and peace twisted her beautiful features into a mask that would scare any grown man right out of his boots. I acted on pure instinct in that moment. Just as I did when I showed up at the lantern ceremony only to walk away and leave her standing there. And every moment after that when my hands went on autopilot to reach out to contact her in some form. I knew that if I ever reconnected with her, I wouldn't be able to let go and allow her the time and space she needed to grieve.

The dominate in me wanted to take control, wrap her up and care for her on a level that no one else could. However, I knew I had to let her go and pray I would be graced with a second chance down the road. When we found each other again, I wanted it to be fortuitous, free of guilt or pain. Yet, it's obvious she still battles with the wounds of loss. I can't say I blame her in the slightest.

Yesterday had been a downright terrible day working for the cheapest man alive. It had been my intention to simply take a break to grab a cuppa before heading back to the office. For no good reason, I had a sense of urgency to go to that very café, and, low and behold, the heavens had fallen straight into the earth in the form of an angel, standing right there, in the flesh.

A little over a year did nothing to dampen her flawless grace and beauty. I couldn't believe my eyes at first, having searched strangers' faces for hers since the moment I turned from her on that beach path. It didn't take long for her quick wit to give me the pinch of needed reality, as well as remind me why I fell so hard to begin with. Hence, pushing her into dinner. Clearly, she attempted to deny what we shared, and she grappled non-stop with wanting to fight it all. Yet, she eventually let go—for me. I'm a simple man, not quite sure why she took to me in the first place, but who am I to question such luck? All I know is this was the best night of my life. Never have I connected with another on this level, not even when fully immersed in the dungeon, and I'll be damned if I let her walk away before we give whatever this is a fair chance. Lord help anyone who attempts to get in my way either.

Splaying my fingers, I encompass as much of her lovely ass as possible with one hand and greedily pull her closer as joy overtakes me. With her beside me, I gaze out the window, watching the stars in peace.

Jade

The early morning rays of dawn dance in through the open curtains as a light breeze gently lifts them, snaking through the room and caressing our bare skin. I barely remember falling asleep, but I awake in his arms.

"Good mornin', sleepy head." His touch expands over my hip before gripping in lust.

"Morning." My leg languidly stretches back over him. I suddenly become inspired to follow it until I come to sit astride, grinding against his morning erection. What can I say? Last night was best I've had. I'll also be packing up as soon as he leaves. I might as well get one more taste of this delicious man. Apparently, the new leaf I have turned is an insatiable one.

"Yes, a very good mornin' indeed." He groans.

Feeling emboldened by God knows what, I take control, claiming his mouth with mine, something unfamiliar and hungry taking over my being. He feels so good, every bit of him. His hands waste no time in their attempt to try to explore, but I take them and playfully pin them over his head. It's kind of a joke seeing that he's double my size, but he allows it, which makes it even better. Within minutes, I have us both worked up, heavily panting and straining for more. With a heavy gasp, I tear my swollen lips away from his, my tongue chasing the remnants of his hot kiss hanging there. The throbbing between my legs is burning me to the core, the yearning to have him deep inside unbearable.

Leaning back with a naughty smirk, I shake the blonde waves out of my face and lift up. Grasping his thick shaft, I position the head right where I want it, right where I need it most, and hover. He thrusts up, trying to maneuver forward, but I hold him at bay. I really have no idea what I'm doing, but he inspires things out of me that I can't explain.

"Mhm, we should probably just go get some breakfast," I breathlessly tease as my hips sway.

"Yer torturin' me," he groans in a scruffy, deep voice.

Pleased with this, I slide down on his dick, taking all of him in one motion. It hurts, no doubt, my shit is super sore, but it is a pain that scratches an itch so deep, I need it again in order to grasp at the edge of feeling alive. He bucks off the bed, fingers digging into my hips as he tries to take over, his dominance prowling just under the surface of his kind demeanor. I lift up and repeat the same motion, the pain searing through my battered pussy, making me see stars. His length had to be that perfect seven to eight inches women talk about, and, aside from this last week, I hadn't had sex in a few years.

On the third downward thrust, something feral consumes me as I ride him like a mad woman. The physical pain, the anger about having to leave him after this, and the pure pleasure all batter me at once, overloading my senses. My hearing fades as hot tears threaten my eyes, and my mind shifts into a sweet numbness.

"Fuck, Jade," Shae moans in the distance, gripping me tighter as he begins to pulsate deep inside, filling me completely.

"Shae!" My fingernails rake down his rock-hard chest as I follow him down the rabbit hole, lost in sensation, wrapped up in all that is this spontaneous, magnificent moment.

It seems to take forever for us to collect ourselves, as if our bodies knew instinctively what I have yet to tell him—that this will be the last time. But, before he can catch on with his spidey senses, his phone vibrates on the nightstand, buying time.

"Sorry, love. I have to get that." He sits up with ease and grabs it even though he is still inside of me with me wrapped around him. "This is Shae." He winks at me as the loud voice on the other end booms through the receiver and elicits a dramatic eye roll from Shae. Not wanting to interrupt, I ease off him, wincing and sucking in a breath as our bodies separate. On my initial attempt at forward momentum, my jelly-like step falters momentarily before I find my ground. Reaching up to the sky, I stretch and give my aching body a moment before I journey forward.

Padding to the bathroom, I close the door, shutting out all the bellyaching ensuing in the distance. I don't think I've ever walked so naked and free in a room in front of another. Normally, my hands frantically search for a robe or a shred of threading. Having been raised up around the naked hippies I call Mom and Dad, clinging to that bit of modesty somehow became a necessity in my childhood. They never questioned me on it; they let me do as I pleased.

Turning the water onto full blast, I slip into the folds of warmth and allow it to envelope my tender flesh. Not wanting to think about the painful separation to come, I simply enjoy the sensations cascading over my body. Grabbing the soap, I leisurely lather up. When my fingers graze the space between my thighs, I realize we didn't use a condom. Fucking Sorcha would be so pissed. It's not like I can get pregnant. Doctors deemed my uterus "hostile" soon after Jack started treatment and gave me a less than one percent chance of ever conceiving. I went privately to be tested without telling Jack, morbid curiosity and all. The timing worked out. Chemo killed his sperm count, which had us looking toward adoption, but we soon tabled it all when we realized the road we were in for. Fuck it, I'll see my doctor and get tested again when I get back, but it's probably fine.

The curtain waves as broad shoulders cast a shadow just on the other side, and Shae's dazzling eyes peek out around the corner. "Can I join ye?"

"Yeah." I smile at him. He really does have a way of lightening my mood.

"Here, let me do that." He grabs the soap from me as he climbs in and affectionately soaps my body, taking special care. Before long, he's washed my hair, cleaned himself, and wraps me in his arms as the water beats down on us.

"Jade, thank ye for the best night of my life." He kisses the top of my head. "I have to head to the job site. My boss is not happy. Can I take ye to dinner tonight?"

Guilt wracks me as my shoulders fold, and I scramble. I can't tell him I'm leaving or he will try to get me to stay, but I don't want to lie to him either. "Why don't you call me when you are off, and we will see? Gavin sorted my same line out so I can use it wherever I go."

His brow pinches as he looks right through me, not liking what he's heard, but he lets it go. "All right." He shuts off the water and fetches our towels, not letting me out until he's tucked me into one. I bat him away and send him to get dressed, completely unused to such tenderness. It is in many ways more intimate than sex.

As he shuffles around the other room, I take a deep breath in of the humid air and wipe the fog from the mirror with my palm. Staring at the haunted reflection, I put on my best fake smile and towel dry my waves briefly before allowing them to fall past my shoulders. The sound of Shae cussing under his breath in the other room makes me smirk as his phone keeps going off on the table.

"Jade, I have to go," he calls out. I give myself one last pep talk and emerge from the steamy seclusion of the bath.

"Okay." I find him by the door, coat in arm, torn dress shirt open in the front for the world to see what is usually hidden. "Sorry about that." My hands automatically try to close his button-less shirt, shielding what a tiny piece of me already feels possessive about.

"Not to worry. I have plenty more back in my room. I'll see ye tonight." It's not a question.

I lift up on tiptoe and kiss his cheek. "Hope you have a good day." Before I can pull away, he is on me, one hand clasped around my back and one laced up through my hair. He graces me with a deep, primal look, and then kisses me hard before quickly pulling back, leaving me breathless. Shae grins, that damn dimple of his coming through. He's completely satisfied with himself as he heads out the door.

Quickly, I shut the portal that just sucked him out of my life and collapse on the floor in my towel. Tucking my knees up under me, I silently hold myself and cry as I flit through the stages of grief all over again, stages I thought I was done with. Why did this have to hurt so badly? I promised Jack I would go on and live enough for the both of us, but I never promised to stop loving him. My soul, my heart, only belonged to one, and that was Jack. Shae is a threat to that as our connection is raw and life altering, I can't have it. I can't have anyone impede on the love in my heart for my lost husband. Tired of my own antics, I find the strength to pick myself up with a new resolve. it's time to get on with living big, as I had promised.

∞

The train's whistle blows in the background, its high-pitched call assaulting ears all around as we wait on the platform to board. The reverberating echo mixes with the bustling of people in a vintage fashion, much like a scene from an old black-and-white film, but set among the more modernized state of things. The unique atmosphere bleeds into the rising summer heat, adding to the irony. Here I sit, a lone woman with a giant suitcase and travel backpack on a bench, alone. But that was my choice, and I'm just going to have to learn how to lie in the bed I made. Flashbacks of last night threaten to consume me as I wait for my train. My cheeks flare as phantom, velvety lips caress my skin, and I try to shake them away. Sure, flying is easier, but I've never done this mode of travel before, and what better way to see the countryside? It's not as if I have time constraints. With a heavy sigh, I nibble on my scone and people watch.

"Is this seat taken?" a gentleman asks, and I shake my head without even looking. The stranger picks up my bag next to me and sets it down so that he can sit right in my personal space. I start to protest, dry crumbs of scone escaping my mouth as I rev up, blinded by his audacity, before I realize who it is.

"How'd—" manages to slip out of my crowded mouth as my jaw goes slack and the blood drains from my face.

"Lass, I know ye better than ye give me credit for. I saw you runnin' from me the minute ye woke. I tailed ye here." Shae wraps an arm around my shoulders and pulls me into the lapel of his suit jacket. His cologne wafts into my next breath, threatening to unlock those tears once more.

"Shae, I'm sorry. I just can't." My voice falters as I force the last bit of food down my throat.

"Jade." He sighs, his hand coming up to brush my cheek and tilt my head up to meet his gaze. "Why ye runnin?"

"I can't do this with you. We don't need to get into it. We had an amazing time together, memorable for sure. Now, it's time to go our separate ways."

"Ye dinnae answer the question." His jawline ticks and his accent deepens as his patience wears thin.

"What do you want? We are just two old friends who had a fling. Let it go." I don't back down.

He sucks in air like I just slapped him. "Is that really what ye think?"

"Am I wrong?" I challenge, my sass finding me well.

"Yes, dead wrong." He growls as anger reddens his cheeks.

"Well, that's all I am good for." I regret it as soon as it slips out.

"Ye really think so little of yerself?"

"Shae, you are a good man. You deserve to spend your time with someone who can give you what you want. I'm not it." A train whistles in the distance, adding to the intensity of our matched wills.

"And what makes ye so sure ye know what I want, ye haven't even asked me," he says.

I swallow hard, not wanting to know the answer, but I can't help but jump headlong into it. "What do you want?"

"I want ye. I want to wake up next to, travel with, eat with, and debate all topics with only ye. I haven't desired or thought of another since that day I left ye standin' on the beach. I should have stayed. I should have been there to catch ye." Now I understand a bit more what I've occasionally seen ghost across in his troubled expressions.

"You don't know me."

"Aye, but I do. And my heart wants what it wants, lass."

"My heart isn't available." There, I said it. Instead of being one of those stupid chicks who can never say what they mean, I did it. Where's my brownie button now?

"I understood that the minute I carried ye from the road I knocked ye out of—that ye might never be able to offer that. I'm not tryin' to compete with a dead man. I'm tryin' to take ye as ye are."

"I'm broken." I sob out of nowhere, the years' worth of tension and trials trying to blast me wide open. I do what I do best—try to fight it.

"Hey now." He takes a handkerchief out of his pocket, dabs my face, and holds me, letting me grapple with my emotions. He guides my head to his shoulder as he attempts to soothe me. "Yer far

from broken, lass. A little weathered, sure, but the best of them are."
His alluring grin comes out, and I can't help but smile back. "I just
found ye again; ye really think I was about to let ye go so easily?"

"I can't help but think you are wasting your time." Surely,
he saw that. I will never love another like I did Jack, and I am barren.
What a flippin' catch.

"Woman, would you let me be the judge of that?" he
smarts, making me fall just a bit further for him in an instant.

"Shae, I can't have kids, and I'm still in love with a dead
man. You are a terrible judge."

"Wow, lass. Yer gettin' a bit ahead of yerself. I ain't
proposin' just yet." His boyish smirk widens to show his perfect
white teeth, a smile that makes it near impossible to be upset. "How
bout we start with going for a cup coffee?" He pulls me further into
him, sensing my need to be as close as possible.

"Shae, my train leaves soon." I half-heartedly attempt to
fight a losing battle. The minute he showed up here, I was done for.

"Where to?"

"Brussels—beer, chocolate, and Belgian surrealism."

"Well, how bout ye stay with me, here, the rest of the week,
so I can finish up with the blowhard givin' me a run. Then we go to
Belgium?"

"Then what? You come with me on all the rest of my stops,
miss work all that time, and then go home to Scotland when I head
back to the US?" It was a bitch thing to say with all my sass-and-
circumstance.

"Why do we have to put a time label on it or constraints?
Why can't we let it be and live in the moment? I make my own

schedule. As soon as my commitments are done here, I am as good as yers."

"For the love of God, this is insane." I sigh and pull back.

"Usually the best ones are." He chuckles to himself

I play smack him on the shoulder. He grabs my hand on descent and brings it to his mouth, tracing kisses along the back, as if knowing how easily his spell can be cast over my will.

"All right. But I have a very full schedule, mind you. There are many places I want to see before I am due back in London," I warn, the need to lay out some form of control taking over.

"Aye, Captain. What's back in London?"

"My friends are all coming over for a holiday in London."

"Ah, a reunion then. I look forward to it."

"Who said you were invited?"

"Oh, I am invited, just ye wait and see." He dips down and claims my mouth, sealing our deal. Lord, what have I agreed to?

∞

Sitting at the little bistro table next to the large window in our hotel suite, I gather my nerve to dial up Sorcha. The sun is beginning its recession from our jam-packed day of touring, which means my grumpy bestie should be rising. Opening the laptop and positioning it right out of the direct sun, I take a deep breath and dial up video chat. The line is picked up from the other side in a whirlwind of grunts and bedding flying by the screen. Big, green eyes and a lion's mane of hair come into view, a bit too close to the screen.

"Really? Your ass is MIA for over a week, and now you decide to call when I am trying to sleep?" Her mouth crooks as she attempts to keep a straight face.

"Bitch, please. It's almost eleven there. You should be up."

"Ugh, this life-sucking leech has me feeling like I have the flu twenty-four-seven." She groans and tries to get comfortable.

"Sorcha," Gavin growls in warning in the background as his huge, looming figure strides into the background. A pillar of strength in her crazy, testy world.

"Hey, Jade." He two-finger waves in the distance, and then saunters off into the bathroom, his muscles bunching through his T-shirt as he goes. She must be on her iPad for me to catch all that. Seeing Gavin in the flesh gives me flashbacks of James, which inevitably leads to more useless guilt. Gavin is quite a bit bigger, and deadlier, but they are brothers for sure.

"Let me guess—you've been calling the baby a leech?" I sigh.

"Well, that's what it is. A vampiric leech sucking the life out of me, ruining every meal I try to eat by inducing immediate emesis following consumption. That big fucker in there can kiss my ass. He did this to me, him and his super sperm," she whines and falls back into her pillows with a soft whoosh, taking the screen with her. For such a vulgar, pissy little thing, she looks quite angelic with her hair spread all about her on the fluffy white pillow.

"You almost look like a saint, glow and all. If it wasn't for your mouth, no one would know better." I chuckle, and she sticks her tongue out at me.

~125~

"Speaking of glow… my, my. You've got quite a bit of color to your cheeks." Her eyes narrow as she scrutinizes my face before smoothing it back out into her unreadable expression. Shit. "Interesting how you left poor James all heartbroken after one night of wild monkey sex only to up and go radio silence on us. If it wasn't for a few selfies you put up, and Gavin tracking you via GPS, we might have gotten worried. So, what's his name?" Man, I feel sorry for Gavin. Lord help him if he ever tries to pull a fast one on her. She can sniff out a rat within seconds.

"It's nothing, just a bit of fun. You don't need to worry." I cough and scoot away from the screen, reaching for my tea.

"If I was worried, I would sick my secret agent of a baby daddy on you." Her brow arches.

Gavin runs on the scary side, that's for sure. I've half expected to run into him around a random corner while abroad. I didn't put it past her to send him my way, or his compliance in her request. He may be the Dom in their relationship, but she runs the show. The man bends over backward for her. She, in turn, spoils him in her own way. She's an impossible nut to crack, except with Gavin. She splits wide open for him. Thank heavens they found one another. I was worried about her becoming the crazy cat lady who loses her ever-lovin' mind. I seriously had visions of hoarders gone wrong in her flat, and having to leave bags of groceries on her doorstep. She's really bloomed in his presence. Sadness nips away at me as I realize how I used to be the vibrant one and she the cynic, and how over the last year, the roles reversed.

"Yo, you gonna tell me what's going on or are we hopping a plane two weeks early?" She snaps my attention back around.

"Remember Shae?" Her face lights up as she blinds me with her smile, her mind quickly working in overdrive, as per usual, lining up all the dots with ease despite the limited information at her fingertips.

"No shit? How the hell did that happen?" She sits back up, giving me visual whiplash, and I have to look away, motion sickness hitting me from the rapid movement.

Knowing full and well I better start spilling the beans, I start from the top. From Prague, to the amazing first night, how I attempted to run away, all the way up to how we ended in Brussels. After I finish confessing like a naughty child in the hot seat, I finally feel as if I can ease back into my seat.

"Oh my God. Samuel, Ben, and Molly are gonna flip. This is freakin' amazing, Jade! Cosmic intervention." She squeals in delight.

"Don't go too far, Sor. Please. We are just having fun."

"Fun, my ass. That man has been stupid in love with you from day one."

"You don't know that. And he already knows that I am not available like that. I was honest from the start," I proudly state, puffing my chest a bit.

"Were you?"

"Yes!" My defensive reply doesn't sit well at all.

"Right. Lie to yourself all you want, Jade. But through sickness and health, I am your bestie, and I will always give it to you straight. You are being stupid."

"Sor, why are you being a bitch?"

"I'm always a bitch. That's nothing new." She shrugs indifferently. "And, do you really think Jack would want you to spend the rest of your life alone, unable to love another because you were still pining after him? I think not."

"Well, glad to know you are his new mouthpiece. I'll just be going." My hand defensively lifts to end the call.

"Jade, wait. Don't shut down and hang up on me."

I pause. "What do you want me to do? Sit here and listen to you tell me how fucked in the head I am?"

"You are a funny bird, highly intelligent and clueless all in one. But I love you and just want the best for you. I wish you could look at it from the outside, love."

"Thank you?"

"It's your journey; I know you will find your way back when it's time." Sorcha looks away from the lens at something coming toward her. Judging by the look in her eyes, it's someone special. Soon enough, Gavin's stern face and whiskey-brown eyes come into view, upside down as he leans over the iPad to see me.

"Ya look good, kid. If you don't mind, I'll be stealin' this one. She has a doctor appointment."

Sorcha groans loudly in the background. "For the love of God, Gavin, women have been having babies for centuries without runnin' to the damn doctor every five minutes." Such a bellyacher, she is.

"Woman, that'll be enough out of you. You are going for your prenatal check-up. If I have to carry you kicking and screaming, and you know I will… and if I have to, you will be looking at some time kneeling in rice," Gavin threatens before moving out of range.

The look on Sorcha's face is priceless, her lips pouting like a petulant child. I know she wants to spew a toe-curling retort, but she refrains, knowing good and well what she'll be in store for. Yes, he handles her well. She needs that firm hand. If left up to her, she'd never go to the doctor and would try to birth that baby at home all by herself.

"Well, guess I better throw on some fat pants." Her bottom lip quivers.

"Fat, yeah." I roll my eyes at her.

"Just wait. By the time you get your ass back here, I will be a proper beached whale."

"Go let your man take care of you. Stop being such a mouthy bitch." I smile at her and blow her a kiss.

"Same goes to you." She gives me this look that eats away to my soul. I try to shake it off.

"Yeah, right. Later."

Unease settles in the pit of my stomach as I look out over the town down below, the perfect pairing of antiquated times meets modern amenities. Brick and stone facades line the streets like weathered lines in an elder's face, the depth of young and vigor hiding within. Europe was beautiful like that, so many ancient secrets littered about, waiting to be discovered. Voices and footsteps of the past echo into the current day. While my teaching schedule will resume come fall, I am in no hurry to get back. I could stay here, lost in these ancient worlds within worlds, tracing the historic lines like fingers across the pages of a book. The last week with Shae has been amazing. We've tasted culinary delights, walked historical sites like Laeken Palace, and he even surprised me with a picnic lunch in the

Bois de la Cambre and Foret de Soignes yesterday. That experience was wonderful, simple wine brilliantly paired with fruit and cheeses, all spread out on a blanket in the middle of a stunning park. We laid there for hours talking and enjoying each other as unhurriedly as aficionados of the world's finest treasures. I sigh contentedly, recalling the events following our dinner. You would have thought it was our first time all over again as we ripped the clothes from each other's bodies before we barely closed ourselves into our room. Paradise.

Chapter 8

Shae

The phone begins to vibrate in my pocket, alerting me to some other dire need when all I want to do is get back to the hotel and my sweet Jade. She had been sleeping quite well; I thought I might catch an hour in the gym. Alas, my assistant had other plans. Apparently, my skillset is needed for some big projects that I can't turn down, a factor placing time limitations I don't quite care to have at the moment. I made it through about fifteen minutes of my run before I had to step outside and mediate yet another call.

"This is Shae," I answer in a clipped tone just as I begin to head back to the locker room, expecting Sue, my assistant, to begin her haggard rampage.

"It's been a long time, my friend." Gavin's deep voice booms out ominously over the receiver.

"So it has," I manage through my surprise, my mind instantly racing through possibilities. We'd always been cordial in passing at the Velvet Rope when I'd come through town on a project, but I purposely kept to myself as I was an out of towner. I knew good and well how some of the Doms at the club could be. Gavin had been an ally of sorts and not someone I was in a hurry to tick off. I roped in the back, kept to myself, and let the rest have at it. When I played, it was about the art and watching it form as I went. Rarely did I care to fuck what I played with like most of the men there, preferring a deeper connection to be in place before any physical intimacy beyond my hands grazing bare skin as they worked. Call me a gentle giant of sorts, I suppose.

"Interesting talk among the women. Sorcha tells me you and Jade managed to find each other again."

"Somethin' tells me this is not new information to ye," I carefully counter, knowing full and well who I am dealing with.

"Jade is essentially my family, the little sister I never had. You didn't think I'd let her run off across the world without some safety features in place?"

"I wouldn't expect anythin' less. To what do I owe this pleasure?" I sigh and run a hand through my messy hair.

"Jade may support our lifestyle, but she certainly doesn't practice it. Have you disclosed your preferences to her?"

"Certainly don't see how that would be a concern of yers, not to be brash."

"Ah, but it is." The tone of his voice tells me where he is going with this, and my reserved normal slips into a more aggressive nature.

"No, Gavin, it is no concern to ye, I understand yer protective nature over Jade but there is no need to go down that road."

"I gave my word I would look after her, and that is precisely what I intend to do. You need to be straight up and honest with her."

"I'd appreciate a bit more respect and confidence if ye will. My intentions are nothin' but pure when it comes to her." My temper is rising as I grit my teeth and try to hold a bit of understanding for where he is coming from.

"I should hope so." He sighs heavily, the tension fleeting from his respective tone.

"Listen, Gavin, she's stronger than ye are givin' her credit for. She certainly isn't made of glass." The woman is a stubborn mule and a bit more adventurous than I had prepared for. Just yesterday, she damn near gave me a heart attack after finding an old bridge that fascinated her to the point of scaling a wall to get a closer look.

"For every ounce of strength you see in her, she has an equal amount of vulnerability. If I remember correctly, it was my home she grieved in for almost a year." A hint of judgement crosses through the receiver.

"Do I sense a touch of an opinion on that matter as well?"

"We may not know each other terribly well, but I know enough to question why you didn't ever come back around. It was clear the moment I saw you with her that you felt more than friendly for her. She could have used someone to be strong for her, someone who actually stood a chance in breaking through her grief."

"Do ye really think I walked away that easily—that it didn't wound me just as deep? Gavin, with all due respect, ye need to think a bit deeper. It's not all brawn and control. The last thin' she needed at that moment was the likes of me chasin' after her as she mourned her beloved. That sure as hell would have complicated matters more." Why does he care? I was a momentary blip back then.

"I didn't mean to try to jump in her pants, Shae, I meant show up as the friend she needed instead of running off with your tail between your legs."

"Fuck off, Gavin. You don't know what you are talking about, in the slightest," I growl, my inner beast now seething.

"Seems I easily hit a nerve and cracked that composed exterior. I want you to remember that. Remember that is a slight scratch in the surface of triggers I can flip should you piss me off when it comes to her," he warns, this clearly all being a game. My, how quickly he picked my insecurities and made them bleed.

"How'd ye know that was the nerve to hit to send your little message?" I try to laugh off the question.

"Please, as if it was hard. You may be on the softer side of some things, but you are a Dom nonetheless. Look, if I thought you were bad for her, she'd never left Prague with you, guaranteed. I do hope you are building foundational communication, heavy in *honesty,* considering your true nature and hers."

I don't know whether to be pissed off or appreciative for his concern, as it is nice to know someone has been looking out for her on this level. "I am grateful for yer concern over the lass, but please, back the fuck off," I warn.

Gavin's laugh booms in the background. "There ya go, that, that right there... never forget it, be honest about it, and we will be just fine. I know your demons, I know your past, and I have a pretty damn good idea on what drives you," he threatens before the line drops.

He truly is the bastard his reputation says him to be. I should have known the indiscretions of my youth would be stamped all over his radar. In all fairness, I was a mess after my mum passed before her time, and my father and grandfather had their work cut out for them. Eventually, I shaped up.

Slapping the swinging door of the locker room door open, I stalk over to my bag and pack up. Jade should be getting up about now, and I don't want to miss a moment with her, especially now that I have a week left at best with her. Jesus, Mary, and Joseph, what the hell am I going to do? She lives halfway around the world from me. I can't move my permanent base from Glasgow even with as much as I travel. Grabbing my water, I throw it into the bottom of my bag with a loud clunk as my head drops back and I close my eyes in prayer. "Fuck, Mum, I've been prayin' for this woman since long before I met her, and now ye have to go slappin' me with the realities I don't want to face." My head falls forward with a sigh as I grab everything and head back up to the room.

I'm lost in my own tortuous thoughts, and my hands work the rooms lock on autopilot. Popping my head around the door, I find her resting peacefully. Her long, blonde hair is angelically fanned out around her tan, bare shoulders. Her skin is ridiculously perfect. My eyes rake her nude, sprawled figure, and my hands begin to itch for rope, while my mind races with possibilities. Never have I bound and fucked a woman at the same time, but God help me, that's exactly the kind of thoughts that have me suddenly hard. Dropping my bag, I shuck my clothes as fast as possible and slowly ease onto the bed. She doesn't need to know about my kink fetishes. Our time together is limited. Honestly, being lost in her softness as much as possible is all that I need to stave off my beast.

When I lightly run a hand up her smooth calf, her body responds to me immediately, even with her being deeply asleep. As my hand travels higher, reveling in her beautiful form and satin skin, she begins to moan, undoing me completely. Without another thought, I ditch my self-control and decide to wake her up with the best morning alarm I can think of.

∞

"Shae, we should get up." Jade's heavenly voice is muffled from our pile of down pillows and entangled limbs.

I groan and pull her closer, not wanting to move a single inch.

"Shae, really, I'm starving." She giggles, lightening me up in a way I can't explain.

"Well, if my queen demands it, I best obey," I joke and pick up a long lock of her tresses, dancing the end of it around her delicate wrist that rests on her stomach. I feel her tense, sending my mind into doubt as I assess what could have triggered it.

"Your queen? A bit much, don't ya think?" she sasses.

"No, it's the truth," I automatically reply.

"Shae, we barely know each other for you to be making such heavy claims."

"Jade, I'd say we've come to know each other quite well," I purr as I dip to kiss her neck, her flesh shivering on impact.

"I don't even know what your favorite color is or something dark about you that you don't tell many people. So, no, we got a ways to go." She sighs, her brain waking up from the sex-induced fog just like that, ready to challenge me once again. It's tempting to drop between her legs to gorge myself on her heaven as well as send us back into the moment we were just carousing in.

"Sweet Jade, will ye ever give it a rest?" I chuckle as I move over her so I can look her straight in the eyes, as well as get a small fill of delight from the flesh-on-flesh contact. The cute scowl now sitting on her brow tells me no. Dropping my lips to smooth that furrowed pinch, I inhale her deeply. "Fine. My favorite color used to be green, but now it is blue and green. Something dark…" I kiss her again, and Gavin's words trickle into the forefront of my mind. Instinct tells me to take it and run, knowing he was right in many ways. "I like some forms of kink."

"Oh? Do tell." Her hands come around to run down my back as I kiss her cheek.

"That doesn't frighten ye?" That is the last thing I intend to do. I'd rather never play again than have her afraid of me.

"Have you met my masochistic best friend and her man? Well, only briefly, I suppose. They are in the lifestyle big time. I'm not down with pain, but I am open to hearing more about what you like," she encourages.

Taking a deep breath, I send thanks for this opportunity to be open with her. "Do ye know what shibari is?"

"Nope."

"Have ye seen pictures of people tied up in ropes?"

"Oh, yeah, Sorcha has shown me. It's quite pretty from an artistic stance."

"I like to be the one to tie others up and form that beautiful knot work."

"Wow." She takes a deep breath. "You want to try that on me?" I am not sure if it is a question or if she is attempting to figure out how she feels about the matter.

"Jade, it's somethin' I enjoy, but it's not a necessity. Would I like to bind ye? Absolutely, but it's not a must." Now my nerves are creeping in.

"I don't think I could ever be into that kind of thing, Shae, but thank you for telling me. I just pray what I can give is enough."

"Please, stop there. Ye are more than I could ever hope for just as ye are, my queen." Before she can contest, my mouth finds hers. Her sweet taste blooms over my tongue as I force it in to penetrate her. I can't get close enough. I feel the tension leave her body as she opens wide for me. A deep groan escapes my chest as the head of my cock brushes the dampness now seeping out from between her legs.

"Shae! I really need to eat; can't we grab a quick bite, and then fall back into this?" she teases, and I can feel her pulling away. Her damn emotional battle continues to rage on. Just as she lets go, she finds a way to cling back onto it. Yet another factor stimulating my doubt on how far this can really ever go.

"All right, ye demandin' lass. Yer lucky we just spent the mornin' doin' just this, or I wouldn't be able to let ye go." I laugh it off and roll away.

"You, sir, are insatiable." She winks and gets up to go to the shower. Watching her walk that way, getting a full-access view to her luscious bottom, I yield to palming up my cock. It doesn't take long before I release a quick one and head to join her in the shower. That woman does things to me I can't explain.

Chapter 9

Jade

I damn near haul Shae up and down the bustling walkways between each set of vendor stalls. Everything is teeming with sights, sounds, and smells that I can't get enough of. This place is amazing. The colors, the people… the very essence of everything wrapped up in this experience has me on a new high. A savory scent drifts in on a slight breeze, forcing my feet to make a hard left, almost sending the large mass in tow toppling as he hadn't expected the sudden change in direction.

"For the love of Christ, woman, where we off to now?" He groans as his long legs catch back up to my fast-moving ones.

"I smell meat," I say as I take a sharp right and stop before a stand overflowing with large vats of paella, chicken, and something I suspect to be seafood based.

"I think yer new nickname should be bloodhound." Shae laughs.

"Would you look at the size of those mussels over there!" I excitedly push past the mass of a man now finding amusement in my love of food, leaving the tall cylinders brewing up something that smells like heaven.

"Which is it? Choucroute or are we goin' to try to figure out how to sauté mussels in our hotel room that doesn't have a kitchenette?" he teases as I stop before a beautiful fresh seafood display.

"Can't we do both?" My fingertips trace the cool glass barrier between the shelled treasures and myself. As the temperature change shifts over my skin, a distant memory seeps into me, one from happier times. About three years ago, I had had a terrible week with work and the dean breathing down my neck for some questionable material I felt the need to teach. A simple insight into sexual revolutions taking place within works of art initially deemed religiously and morally sound. So shoot me for thinking outside of the box. My mood had been downright terrible, and I had come home to Jack. He was cooking my favorite mussel dish in white wine while blasting some funky blues music. I hadn't expected him home; he had been pulling many late nights in the office. He met me by the kitchen island, took my coat and bag, set them down, and then pulled me close and made me dance with him. He always knew when I needed to dance away my stress. The memory of his cologne as he had held me tight stings my eyes as I shift back into present time.

"Never mind, let's go back to that chouc-whatever." I turn on a dime, rushing back toward the oncoming man who's been by my side the last week or so, trying to get as far as possible from the apparitions of my past and their phantom pains I can never seem to fully escape.

"Are ye all right, lass?" Shae's gaze narrows in on my damp eyes.

"Yup, totally fine. Now, tell me what this stuff tastes like." My chin lifts toward the steaming delectable dish simmering close by.

"I don't know why ye won't just talk to me." Shae sighs in exasperation, placing a hand on my shoulder, trying to hold me in place.

"We talk all the time, about everything."

"Everythin' but what ye are feelin'. Why won't ye open up to me?" The pain I have been unknowingly causing him becomes quite evident, adding yet another blow to the torrential downpour attempting to brew inside.

"Shae, you didn't do anything wrong. It has nothing to do with you at all. I don't want you taking my stuff on."

"Do ye have any idea what it's like for me to lose ye in a single moment? To watch ye go from vibrant to the verge of tears on a flash and not be able to do anything about the obvious pain ye are still in? It is fuckin' maddenin'. I want to take the hurt away but can't, which is about as good as drivin' a dagger into my heart," Shae spits out, the veins in his neck slightly bulging from a temper I didn't know he had. My natural instinct has my form recoiling, something that chases away the demon I had just seen as his face falls. "Forget it, I'll see ye back at the hotel. I gotta take a walk." And just like that, he turns and does just that. Walks away from me and my madness.

A natural reaction would be to run after him, cry, profess my undying affections, beg him to forgive me... but I am not capable of doing any of those things. Tucking it all back into my emotional vault, I order some food and walk to a bench to sit and eat. Every time the guilt or reactionary emotions attempt to surface, I shove them back into the vault that I don't plan on touching with a ten-foot pole.

When I left Prague to go to Belgium with him, I swore I wouldn't cry over anything between the two of us again. This was temporary fun, a bit of adventure within my ongoing adventure in an attempt to find myself again. He is simply a stop along the way, gifted to me. He is amazing, but we can't fool ourselves into thinking it is anything more than temporary. I'm sad that Shae is emotionally invested to the point that he is. Caring as much as he apparently does only makes our impending separation worse.

My heart weighs heavy as I scrape the bottom of my paper cup and toss it into the trash with a bit more gusto than I should have. The crumpled mass topples across the top of the trash before landing on the ground. Bending down with a huff, I snatch it up with an attitude, pissed at the thing for not cooperating. As I ascend, my eyes travel down the little road just beyond the market and settle on an artistically drawn sign for a tattoo shop. The intricately drawn mehndi designs working hard to form the business name within the negative space entrances me further. An old memory of when Jack and I got drunk in college and drew all over each other's legs with henna instead of studying for finals sits on the fringes of my delicate mind. My heart lurches in my chest as my feet continue to walk that way, my mind lost in another repressed memory. For the last year, I had worked so hard at shutting it all out for fear of pain. But, as it would happen, the more I try to move forward in my life, the more present the memories become.

Coming to stop before the window of the shop, mesmerized by the beautiful drawings just on the other side of the window, something makes my hand take the door handle and launch myself into the space. A friendly woman with long, jet-black hair dressed in a retro wiggle dress warmly greets me in French.

"Hi, I don't speak French," I mumble and look at my shoes, wondering what the hell I am up to. Sure, I can order food in French and decipher famous Parisian works of arts names, but that is about it.

"No problem, English it is. How can I help you?" The switch is as fluid as most in this city, making me grateful yet a little ashamed I don't speak another language.

"I'm not quite sure. I saw the beautiful art and came in. I haven't been brave enough to get my first tattoo yet. I don't know how this works," I state as my eyes dance around the paintings hanging on the wall to the left of her.

"Well, we can have you meet with the artist. You can tell him what you have in mind, and he can draw up a custom tattoo. If you don't want to do that, you can take a look through these and just pick one." She pushes a stack of albums toward me with pre-drawn images.

"Mind if I look for just a bit?"

"Not at all." She hops back on her stool and flips through a magazine as my fingers peruse through the pages, looking for God only knows what.

When I hit a nautical-themed section, my heart begins to race as flashes of sailing with Jack hit me. It doesn't hurt like one might think. They are bittersweet, a nice surrender. My fingers stop at a rather masculine-looking compass, and I can hear Jack's voice in my mind. "Good Lord, wife. I think I need to add a compass and GPS tracker to everything you own, including you." My adventurous nature that was constantly enthralled with everything led me astray quite often. I lost things or got lost constantly. The echo of my rebuttal in that moment comes through, a line I used more than once. "Don't worry so much, I'm a grounded, stable, able-bodied woman, like I have a natural, invisible anchor… and I always find a way back."

My eyes mist over as the irony of that memory worms its way in. Thinking of who I used to be before cancer ruined my life and who I became after cancer was dangerous water to tread. I hated the woman with sunken, hollow eyes looking back at me every morning after Jack died. It ate away at me even more than the fucking disease that robbed me. Making this trip happen was a desperate plea to find what once was. My skin begins to pinprick in realization. What was once lost is now slowly being found. Holy mother of God, maybe I am strong enough to find my back. It is then that resolve takes over. Picking up my phone, I text Shae.

I'm sorry for hurting you. I really appreciate you more than you know. I am about to do something crazy. Want to join me?

That's the best I can do for him. I hit send and pray he even answers back. Within minutes, he does.

Aye, ye crazy woman, what are we up to?

Come down to the little tattoo shop just across the way from the mussel stand.

Well, this could be interesting. Be right there.

My heart swells just knowing he is willing to ride in my crazy bus. I excitedly turn to the lady, who is now looking at me with a grin.

"You've decided then?" she guesses.

"Yes, I'd like something custom though."

"Not a problem. Let's go see Diesel." She shoves off the stool and heads to a back workroom.

My heart races in excitement and nervousness as I briskly follow.

When we walk to the back, an antiseptic odor hits my nose as I curiously follow my fearless leader into the unknown. Seated in a workroom, leisurely propped up against a lighted drawing table, a burly biker-looking man tracks us as we approach. The receptionist says something in French to the man, and he stands to take my hand in greeting, kissing the top in a lingering hello that doesn't sit quite right, but I shake it off.

"And what will we be putting on this lovely skin today?" he asks as he traps my suspended hand in his, the pad of his thumb stroking my skin slowly before he lets me go.

"I'd like a compass with an anchor please. But done a bit more feminine."

Diesel, I'm assuming, strokes his long beard in thought before motioning back toward the area we just came from.

"Where would you like it?"

Jeez, I hadn't thought of that. Quickly shuffling through possibilities in my mind, I begin to get a bit anxious. I've always appreciated other people's tattoos, the art drawing me into deeper questioning into their psyche, but I hadn't quite got as far as imagining my own. Seeing me struggle, he blows out a hard breath,

"First one?"

"Yeah."

"How big you thinking?" A twinkle sparks in his eyes.

"Well, I don't want it huge, but big enough to tell what it is, I suppose." Tiny tattoos are cute, but it is sometimes hard to see what's going on unless you are right up on the person. I like wrist placement, upper arm too, but that doesn't seem quite right. The remnants of the last memory creep into the recesses of my mind, Jack's voice coming through strong. "Yeah, an anchor, thank God for that, because the wind is always at your back, blowing you to who knows where."

"I know. How about here?" I lift my hand and pat the back of my shoulder. What the hell, it'd be cute there too.

"Easy. Go have a seat, please." He quickly disengages and turns back around to his table, removing some stencil paper. Hesitantly, and a bit put off how quickly I was dismissed while embarking on a big adventure such as permanent art, I turn back around and head to that area.

Waiting… what a mental game when knowing something scary and exciting is coming down the pipeline. I heard these damn things hurt. What if he starts and I can't sit through the whole enchilada because of the pain? I'll be stuck with some awkward lines that resemble more of a tumor. I begin to nibble on my short nails as I consider talking myself out of it. *No, Jade, sit your ass still and wait to see what he draws first. If you hate it, then run.*

That rationale sits better, the emergency exit plan giving me a tad bit of comfort. In reality, a little bit of pain in the short term is nothing compared to the pain I would experience living with a terrible piece of art inked into my skin. Time slowly ticks by as I wait, and I begin to worry. Does it normally take this long? Glancing at my watch, I realize it has only been about twenty minutes. That's not that long to wait for a custom piece. A movement on the other side of the front window catches my eye as a tall, handsome ginger pulls open the door and locks onto me.

"Shae!" I jump up and animatedly move to embrace him, happy for his calm energy when I am about to crawl out of my skin.

"Well, perhaps absence does make the heart grow fonder. Ye've never greeted me like that before. I like it." His classic, boyish smirk entices my own to reciprocate.

"I'm happy to see you. I don't know how people do this. It is nerve wracking." I blow out a hard breath and sit back down.

"Nah, it's therapeutic."

"I don't see how."

"Just wait until ye are in the seat, deep breathin' through the pain." His brow rises as if to test my reaction. Naturally, he may be a bit reserved, but he is a Dom nonetheless, of course. I still haven't allowed myself to think much about that. None of it has ever held any interest for me. Then again, I've recently found how bold I can really be during lovemaking with this man. The way he embraces all of me and encourages me to let go is otherworldly. I feel my cheeks flush in memory.

"Mhm, what brought that on?" His thumb traces my cheek as hunger strikes his eyes.

"Oh… nothing," I lie.

"Uh-huh," he calls my bluff and sits. It is then Diesel comes from the back, his eyes taking Shae in as a threat before smoothing back out.

"All right, what do you think about this?" Diesel holds out the template. A bold nautical compass with delicate details proudly stares back. A rope dances from the side, leading down to a pretty anchor. I never knew an anchor could be portrayed as pretty, but perhaps it was the piece as a whole. It felt perfect, just right. Tears threaten my eyes as I am rendered speechless.

Discomfort crosses his face. "I'm going to take that as a yes. Follow me, please." He turns on the heel of his leather boot as we jump up to quickly follow. Clearly, he is the type to not wait for anyone. Right behind the reception area, separated by Japanese folding screens, a few different chairs and a massage table are neatly set about at different stations.

"I will place it on your skin first, have you check placement, and then we will start. Please slip your arm out of your top." He throws an odd look at Shae, who has now tightly crossed his arms over his chest and stands protectively near. Moving down the spaghetti strap of my tank top, I let it fall back and turn around so that he can have full access to my bare shoulder. He wipes the area down with something cool, and, to my surprise, he shaves the skin with a throwaway razor. Interesting. Letting it go, I wait for him to finish pressing the paper against my skin.

"All right, have a look in the mirror." His accent deepens as his hairline rises in anticipation.

After walking to the full-length mirror, I turn and peer over my shoulder to view it. Placed perfectly centered within my shoulder blade, and about the size of an orange, the outlines proudly stand out, making me giddy.

"Perfect!"

Diesel's shoulders relax and he motions to a massage chair, the kind where one sits forward with their face in the headrest. "Have a seat. And I guess you can sit there," he mumbles to Shae while flippantly motioning toward a parlor chair close by before turning his attention toward me. As he explains his set up and a few tips to handle the application as well as communicate with him any issues or need for a break, Shae defiantly drags the parlor chair over without asking and sits right in front of me. Diesel goes to say something but stops. I'm betting Shae pulled out one of his looks.

"All right, ready?" Diesel asks.

"Do it." I brace myself. I hear the buzz of the tattoo gun fire up as his gloved hands press into my back to hold me where he wants. As the needle kisses my flesh, I tense against the burn and take a deep breath in. I feel Shae entrap my hand in his and hold me as I attempt to acclimate to the pain. It isn't entirely unpleasant. As he outlines the piece, some areas are more sensitive than others, and I have to force myself to breathe while other sections don't feel like much at all. Overall, I have to admit, I kind of like the feeling. After about ten minutes, I find I have the strength to speak, much of the anticipatory angst leaving my body.

"There ye go, lass. Not so bad now, is it?" Shae quips and releases my hand.

"Nah, not bad at all."

Another breath slowly escapes my body as Diesel carries on, cordially asking us a few questions here and there about our trip, attempting to be a bit more friendly than he had initially. Eventually, he gets lost in his work and leaves the lighthearted chatter up to Shae and me. We never seem to run out of things to talk about. He has an interesting perspective on the world, making even the most mundane topics fascinating to chew over. Then, as is our norm, time rushes forward, and, in no time, Diesel's machine stops.

"All done, you sat brilliantly. Have a look."

I slowly sit up and stretch before hurrying to the mirror. Love at first sight might be a bit over the top, but that is the only way I can think to describe it. It is perfect, holds more memory and meaning than any of those pre-drawn tattoos ever could. Now, in an instant, I can completely understand why these things are so addicting.

"Diesel, I absolutely love it!" I squeal and run over to embrace the big bear in a tight hug. He hadn't anticipated my quick movement and awkwardly stands there, stiff as a board, before lightly patting my other shoulder.

"You are most welcome. Let's get you wrapped up."

After exiting the shop hand in hand, we stroll back toward the market that is now closing up for the evening. I want to rip the plastic off my back and sport my new ink. It is all that I can do to resist. Diesel said I needed to wait a few hours, and he sure knew better than I did.

"Well, should we feed ye now?" Shae jokes and lightly squeezes my hand.

"Oh yes, I hadn't realized how long that took."

"He did a fab job," Shae responds with a hint of discomfort.

"Yeah, his mannerisms were odd, but his art was perfect."

"Odd is one word for it," Shae disgruntledly replies. It seems the two weren't quite fond of each other. Who knows why? "Ye feel okay?" Shae quickly changes the subject.

"I feel fantastic. Wonderfully light." He was right; the experience was quite therapeutic.

"Told ye." He laughs a delightful, deep sound that triggers my body to draw closer to his. "Careful, any closer and we are skippin' dinner," he warns as I slip a hand into his back pocket.

"How about we swing by the deli for a quick bite on the way back to the hotel?" I squeeze his backside through the pocket.

"Yer a terrible influence. Let's go." He steals my hand from his behind and wraps it around his firm bicep before dragging me down the alley toward our hotel. The take-charge tone of the moment sparks a new excitement as my heart flutters, ready for another passion-filled night. He's quickly cemented himself as an addiction that I am not quite sure if I am okay with or not.

We are coming up on the deli at a fast pace. Shae is a man on a mission. I have to slow and pull back on his hold when I see an artist set up under the street lamp, sketching under the fading daylight. The older gentleman resembles my dad, decked out in a linen outfit and a little beret, his weathered hands furiously devouring the paper with each skillful strike of his charcoal. The world around him has stopped, all he can see is the vision in his head attempting to manifest onto the paper. I know that drive, that focus, and that hunger. Some of my best childhood memories were sitting side by side with my dad, each of us with an easel or pad of paper, symbiotically creating from a place of pure passion. Something within me shifts, and my fingers ache to be rolled in charcoal.

I haven't picked my art up since Jack died. It seemed that my passion died with him. Letting go of Shae, I allow my hands to fall to my side as I stand just behind the artist, absorbing the energy from the moment, marinating in it, allowing it to stoke something I thought to be lost.

"You like?" the old man asks, startling me from my trance, my eyes quickly finding his kind ones now patiently waiting for me to respond. My mouth guppies a moment as I scramble for an excuse as to why I rudely invaded his space.

"I'm so sorry." I clasp my hands.

"Not to worry, it must have spoken to you strongly. That is a compliment." He smiles kindly.

"It's stunning; I haven't picked up my pencils in…" I trail off, transfixed by the insane realism of the beautiful woman coming to life on the paper.

"Ah, when she passed, it took me a few years to embrace it again." His eyes take me in with compassion, and then turn back to his work.

"I… yeah. Who is she?" A shiver runs through me, not quite okay with how he was able to deduce that fact so easily.

"My daughter. Drunk driver stole her from me. She speaks to me every day." Sorrow sweeps through his being before his hands find their way back to the paper.

"She was beautiful. Thank you for sharing." He tips his head but says nothing else.

Turning around, I find Shae regarding us intently, yet trying to give us space. Taking his hand, I give him a smile and head toward the little deli's door.

"Miss?" the gentleman calls over his shoulder. I turn back around, poised halfway into the doorway.

"Don't ever let it go again. Once it re-roots in your soul, keep creating even through the pain."

I absently nod as the words hit me deep.

"Thank you." I nod and pull Shae into the shop, not sure how to process and if I really care to at this time. Is that what happened? My need to create is slowly coming back? Does that mean I am healing? Do I really want that to happen? Thoughts whirl as my emotions buck under the waves.

"Ye all right?" Shae zones in, pulling me close, forcing me to look him in the eye.

"I'll be fine. Where were we? I'm hungry." I nestle my face into his chest, the soft fabric mingling with his cologne, comforting me.

"I thought for food?" His voice deepens, and the hand running down my back gets rougher.

"Argh! Yeah, but let's make that quick because I'm more hungry for dessert." He groans, gently pushing me back so that he can approach the counter and order our usual.

While I stand there, my thoughts shift from darkness into the lust-filled night we are about to have. His calm, patient, and open nature has drawn another side of me out that I didn't know existed. In his presence, I bloom. I open wide and feel powerful, sexy, and whole. It pains me to say but even in Jack's presence, my insecurities nipped at my heels. I always tried to hide bits and pieces of my imperfections from him. Shae wouldn't let me; he coaxed a level of freedom from my soul that was authentic and liberating all in its own. I equally loved and felt guilty as hell about that. Fuck, I am broken.

"Ready?" he asks expectantly, holding out a hand, a bag of our treats suspended in the other. Forgoing another dance in the realm of guilt-ridden thoughts, I take his outstretched offering and hold tight, thankful we at least get to have another night together.

Chapter 10

Jade

"You what?" My fork scrapes across my plate as I try to swallow what he just said.

"I have to leave ye a bit early. I can come long enough to spend a few days with ye in London, but then it's back home. I'm so sorry, lass." Shae's beautiful eyes silently plea for something beyond what he is voicing.

This sucks. I'm not ready to let go, to end our time together, not yet. "Well, I understand, if ya gotta go, ya gotta go." I shrug, but, inwardly, my selfish side is screaming for me to kick, beg, and claw into a way to keep us together.

"I thought ye might say that." He looks down at his food as if it is now spoiled.

"What else am I supposed to say?" I scoff.

"Oh, gee, I don't know... perhaps somethin' along the lines of 'that's terrible, I'm disappointed, and I'm going to miss ye'. Somethin' that tells me my absence affects ye at all, or even a compromise on your behalf such as tryin' to come to Scotland for a wee bit," he spits, his temper flaring from thin air, something he is apparently quite well versed in keeping hidden.

"Jesus, is there something else you aren't telling me with that temper of yours?" I quickly change the subject as my fingers grip the tablecloth of our little bistro set in our hotel room. I'm not afraid of what he might do to me; he'd never hurt me. I'm afraid of my own emotions and the direction they are attempting to go against all logic. *We've talked about this, Jade. You can't go with him.*

"No, not at this time. I think I've said enough." Shae abruptly stands. His thick hands clench and unclench before moving to shove up the sleeves of his shirt, flashing the trailing ink. "I'm headed to the gym." He casts one more pained look my way and storms off, gym bag in hand.

Stunned, I use the fork still captured between my fingers to push around a lone strawberry on my plate. I feel a bit of a bond with the damn lone berry. I don't even know what to do with what just happened. Where is this anger coming from again? He's definitely not telling me something. It's not that I feel unsafe around the man, but I need to know if he has a sordid past with that little temper and if I should be worried. Perhaps it would be best to call Sorcha and Gavin? Stabbing the damn strawberry, I pop it into my mouth and make my way into our room to find my laptop. After digging it out of my bag, I slam it down on the table, unsure who I am the most upset with, and fire it up with every intention of calling Sorcha to have that pit bull of hers do some digging.

Before I can get too far, my video chat shows a missed call attempt from my sister, Ruby, and my anger becomes deflated. I haven't talked to her or the kids for weeks and miss them terribly. Feeling my anger dissipate, I call her back, the need to see my sister becoming greater than my desire to tear into the past of a man who clearly doesn't want that drudged up. After a few rings, the screen finally jumps to life, Ruby's long, brown waves falling into view as her face is turned to the background, yelling at a few towhead blurs scattering about. I smile. My nieces and nephew are quite the handful. Their "oh shit, we better run!" squeals of joy echo through the house as they scamper from my sister's threats of no desert after dinner until they clean up the mess they made. She turns back to me with an irritated sigh.

"What did they do and was Max the ring leader again?" I snicker.

"Don't you laugh Miss 'I'm on an exotic vacation while my sister gets her ass handed to her.' Yes, Max thought it would be a grand ole time to lead the girls in a remodeling of sort in the living room." She sits down at the kitchen island, her body almost collapsing on the stool.

"Hey now, I seem to remember someone encouraging me to run away and live for the both of us." I chuckle. She was the biggest push into this trip.

"Yeah, I should have made it a stipulation that you took me with you. So, how's it going?" Ruby's big, brown eyes plead for any distraction I can offer. She's an amazing mother, but a worn-out one. Thankfully, her husband is able to easily afford her to stay home with those rugrats. He's also tried to get another one out of her, but that's never going to happen, Lilah, the baby, damn near did her in with postpartum depression, and she ran to get her tubes tied the minute he mentioned a fourth. Lilah is now five, and Ruby told him he could have a puppy the next time the baby bug bit him. Ruby has well recovered, and we, as a family, swooped in that first year to help every single day. Whether it was housework, childcare, respite time for her, anything she needed, we handled it. Once Lilah turned one, she slowly began to kick us all out. We still help whenever she needs, but she's more than found her footing and is one badass mom.

"I'm good." The weight of my early-morning spat weighs heavy on my words.

"So, you gonna tell me what's really up or do I have to pry it out of you? You know we have about ten minutes before someone touches someone else or takes a toy and all hell breaks loose in there." Her head tips toward the living room.

"Remember Shae?"

"The coffee dude?" She looks intrigued.

I quickly delve into a Reader's Digest version of the last few weeks. Ruby knows me well enough to fill in the blanks. After recapping this morning for her, my traitorous eyes begin to dampen in frustration.

"Seriously, you got your first tattoo without me?" Ruby feigns a hurtful expression.

"After all of that, that is what you have to say?"

"What do you want me to say? I know how hardheaded you are. You see things the way you want to see them and have a hard time looking outside of that lens, just like dad. You are gonna have to figure it out for yourself."

"Would you just say it, please, and let me be the judge of that?"

"Fine, you're an idiot. You are obviously in love with the guy and can't accept it. Like I said, no one can force you to let go of Jack and accept Shae. That's on you." She shrugs, the bags under her eyes darkening.

"Why are you the bitchy one?"

"Someone had to take the role of realist. Mom and me hold it down in that department."

"You're wrong, you know."

"About?"

"Me being in love with him. I care a great deal about him, but that's it. He's just a friend."

"Sure, whatever helps you sleep at night."

"Seriously!"

"Seriously, you are. You are just too blind from your grief. Let Jack go. We can't change that. Trust me, Jade, if I could change that entire situation, I would have at the drop of a dime just to see you smile again, just to take the pain away from you. And if this guy has found a way to light you back up? I'll fight for him to stay too."

"I don't want to talk to you anymore," I pout.

"Don't give me that face. Go pick up your charcoal, draw something, and get over it." She smugly laughs.

"How are Mom and Dad?" The homesickness she inspired is spreading.

"They miss you a lot and wonder why you aren't calling them."

"Because I just needed a break from everyone. I barely talk to Sorcha either—a choice I've paid dearly for already." I love my parents, but they dote worse than everyone else. It makes it impossible to think with their smothering influence.

"Yeah, I bet she's let you know about it. You really need to call Mom and Dad. But seriously, why do you have to come home right after London? You could easily go to Scotland for a week before classes start and have some crazy highlander fantasy most women could only ever dream about."

"We back to that already?"

"Yup."

"Because, Ruby, it's getting harder and harder to conceptualize leaving him, and that's a problem. He's a good man who deserves someone who can actually love him to the full capacity that he deserves. I am not that woman."

"You're not that woman or you are choosing not to be that woman?"

"You think this is a choice?"

"It's absolutely a choice. You choose whether or not you let go, as well as if you are going to open up to receive an obvious gift."

"I didn't choose to fall in love with Jack, and I didn't choose to lose him either!" I spit, my temper trying to burst through my reasoning. Ruby doesn't mean to upset me. What she says is out of love, but it hurts nonetheless.

"God help me. If you weren't a few thousand miles away, I'd slap you. True, but you can choose what happens from here. Trust me, as your extremely jaded and tired sister, run straight for what you want and don't be ashamed of it. I want to see you infused with joy again, Jade. I'm living my dream; there's nowhere else I'd rather be then right here. You deserve that too." The kids start yelling in the background, and she grins before turning to see what happened. "Looks like I have to go, Peanut."

"Oh, don't you even call me that!" I scowl at my hated childhood nickname. As I was the smallest of everyone in my family, my grandparents made it stick quite early on. I hated being the runt.

"All right, Peanut, don't get all roasted on me. Love ya!"

"Ruby!" I yell before she laughs her ass off and quickly ends the call before I can get another word in. Such a bitch. I rub at my chest, trying to ease the burn from her words about Shae now resting there.

My heart continues to ache as I sit back in my chair. We were supposed to tour the Louvre today. Now, I am not sure when he will be back. Or if should I even be here when he does. Shoving off from the table, I throw on my jeans and a comfy pair of shoes before slinging my purse over my shoulder. I can't go to the Louvre without him. He was really looking forward to us experiencing that together. Well, he's already been, but he wanted to take me for my first time. It feels like an asshole move just to go. My feet need to move, though. My spirit is restless.

As I hit the door, my eyes catch my old messenger bag leaning against the desk. Before I know what's happening, my feet turn on a dime, my hands sling the bag over my shoulder, and I am off.

Shae

My feet heavily pound the belt of the treadmill in a rhythmic beat, left foot, right foot, left foot, right foot... as fast as my form can maintain. The mechanical function of a body in motion is a work of art in itself. The second one foot grips the tread, it flexes, rolling the impact from my heel to my toes, springing my body forward, bringing the next step, the rest of me fluidly adapting to follow the overall goal. Stress bunches through my flexed muscles as I force my body to comply with the task at hand. Through this controlled release, I am hoping to work some of the frustration and pain out.

When I fought in the underground circuits, it was purely to release my anger over my mother's early death. I had been a hothead at eighteen, well, my whole life really, but my mum used art therapy to rein me in. She'd pinch pennies and pick up odd job whenever she could to keep me entrenched in all things art. I began scrapping in the schoolyard early on. Somehow, she instinctively knew what to do. My father had been at a loss, his attempts at exercise and sports the only non-impactful answer he had. My mum had been the one with the patience to get through to me. She helped me learn how to temper the rage, how to therapeutically embrace it, and then coalesce into something beautiful. Sweat pours down my body, dripping from every direction, coming to fall like raindrops on the machine I am abusing as I swipe it out of my eyes.

When she passed, I lost my connection to my outlet. I lost my way entirely and set out on a mission to use my fists to rearrange faces in a whirlwind of raw, guttural emotion. At the time, it felt like an act that I had to governor over in the face of feeling completely out of control, utterly powerless. It wasn't until my granddad stepped in that I started to realize the only control I had in this world was over my own actions and how there was a ripple effect happening with every move I made, like a stone being cast over open water.

My granddad is a fisherman and sailor of sorts, with a godly amount of patience. After my first arrest, my father gave me two choices. I could either stay locked up for my two-year sentence or he'd get me a lawyer to try to negotiate an early probation with the judge if I agreed to spend those two years working the wharf, sailing and fishing with my grandad. It is there that I became fascinated with tying knots, but it wasn't until years later that Shibari came into the picture by way of a mate in grad school. My grandad had many passions that bridged me back into my own, back into reconnecting with myself. It is because of him that I went to college. His love of academics rubbed off on me during our time on the sea together.

That is why this blasted woman is so damn infuriating. She refuses to plant two feet firmly back on this plane, leaving one dragging in the past, syphoning from the well of pain that should be laid to rest. I've been on both sides; I've known the struggle, the consuming darkness of hopelessness. And just as she seems to take my hand and come forward, she retracts back into it. She's too luminous, not meant for this world, yet nothing seems right without her. *Fuck!* I scream in my head and hit stop on the machine, my legs trembling and threatening to cramp, unable to go on any further. Glancing at the screen, I see that I only managed five miles.

Jumping off, I swig from my water bottle and head to stretch. The weights are going to have to come tomorrow. Jade's probably waiting for me, and I've already done her a disservice by taking off in the manner I did with no explanation. Rarely does my temper peak these days, but what I feel for her has had a way of altering me in ways I wasn't quite prepared for. With a defeated sigh, I grab my bag and head back up to the room, fully prepared to disclose whatever it is she wants to know. Who am I kidding? The woman owns me heart and soul. I'd lay my life at her feet should she demand it.

Pausing at the hotel door, I hover my hand over the handle before hesitantly opening it to face the mess my temper has once again made. Expectantly, my eyes dart around, searching for the only work of art worth resting my gaze upon. My heart sinks into the pit of my stomach when I see that she has gone, her satchel as well. Rushing to the closet and throwing open the door, I breathe a sigh of relief when I see all of her belongings still there, telling me she just took some time to herself. As much as it pains me, I can live with her taking a day to herself, even though my selfish side feels a bit robbed, wanting all the time that I can manage with her. Falling face first onto the bed, I collapse, unable to shoulder any of it another moment.

Jade

Leaning back in my little cafe chair, I sip my coffee and look over the laid-out sketchbook before me. My eyes trace the lines ebbing and flowing across the cream-colored page, formulating the full figure of a curvy woman. Her arms are outstretched, above her head, tangling themselves in swaying vines. The tree vines separate just enough at the top for a full moon to peek through as if they are drawing back like curtains. As my mind filters through the details and my hands painstakingly take time to add on their own accord, I realize a few odd things. One, she looks a bit bound by the vines. A detail I hadn't intended. Then again, my art truly manifested on its own. I get a flash of an image of what I want to embark on, and the rest follows suit. I am only semi-conscious of what takes place. Was it a metaphor for my past, my present, or my possible future?

My free hand comes up to embrace my engaged forearm clutched to the cooled cup, my mind wondering briefly about the kink Shae is passionate about. He'd never hurt me, and I've been quite pleased with all that he's introduced me to thus far. I can't lie. The thought of being artfully restrained, completely open for his will, makes me clench my thighs in anticipation. Shaking off the spell attempting to cast itself over me, I focus back on the drawing and attempt to delineate the deeper meanings my subconscious is attempting to relay.

"Wow, Miss, that is gorgeous. A little sad, though, no?" A woman stops next to me on her way into the cafe. I hadn't realized anyone else was watching. The startled state of my heart takes a moment to calm before I can answer through my embarrassment.

"What do you see?" I try to slide my teacher hat into place, gaining my footing back as I delve into how art might be moving another soul and wanting to know all about it.

"A beautiful woman being held back by something that haunts her."

"Thank you. I'm not quite sure what to think of it yet."

"Your hands are talented, Miss. Have a good day." She smiles and heads in.

Not wanting to dwell another moment and completely enthralled with my spark flaring back to life, I continue. I want to ride this as long as I can and don't want to look back. Taking the last large gulp from my cup, I greedily trap my pencils and flip the page so I no longer have to look at the woman. Time seems to slow as the meeting of my weapon of choice glides over the blank canvas, eagerly awaiting the strike. The sun rises higher in the sky above me, the radiating heat the only telltale sign as temperature, hunger, and all bodily concerns fall silent as my hands become possessed. Stress and emotional overloads from the early morning melt away as my conscious becomes clear, my viewpoint shifting into a higher state no longer rooted in ego or pain. Being up here is like looking at the world or current issues as if they are a map. All roads leading up to a point of interest and away from it, all clearly laid out in perfect harmony. Wouldn't it be nice if I could view my lives in the same fashion? A road map with clear directions on where to go when I veer off course.

Suddenly, my new tattoo aches, reminding me of its presence, shifting my thoughts as my hands continue their plight. I may not be able to see the future, but I have an anchors to remind myself of where I come from, where my roots and authenticity lie. That way, when the world shifts on axis, no longer makes sense or even appears hostile at times, I can hold true to my foundational being. I've missed her—the old me. Jack's death made me feel as if I had to distance myself from who I really am. That it was disgraceful and selfish to keep being her. In reality, perhaps I committed the biggest sin against myself in doing so.

Early on into Jack's treatment, a part of me knew he was probably not going to make it. I didn't want to accept that truth. I wanted the percentages of survivors and all the hard facts that kept hitting me in the face to be wrong. I wanted the doctors and nurses to be wrong. One day, I wanted them to rush in to tell us it was all a mistake. That they read the tests wrong, and Jack was going to be with us for many years to come.

There's this hallmark scene I had even created in my head, a story I kept on replay. We'd be sitting there on the hospital bed, curled up, watching a movie and making fun of the characters. Then a light knock would sound on the door, making my heart skip a beat, prematurely anticipating more bad news. The door would swing open and a team would swarm in, anxious hands gripping rolled-up papers and whatnot as they circled around us. My voice would catch in my throat, and I'd be at a loss for words as Jack wrapped his arms around me. Then, just when we thought all hope to be lost, the lead white coat would tell us about the mistake. I'd make them repeat it a few dozen times as it sank in. Then I'd scream in delight and jump on Jack, peppering him with kisses and rambling God knows what. The whole scene plays in my head from to top to bottom, an ancient ghostly façade I had built as a coping mechanism. Even the nasty, too-clean smell of the hospital mixed with the stringent bite of constant antibiotics clouding the room stings my nose from memory, something that hasn't happened since I shut off after the funeral.

Tears begins to fall onto my sketchpad, interestingly enough however, they weren't derived from the overwhelming sense of loss like once before. These feel more like a release, an acceptance of sorts, as if something has shifted ever so slightly within my being. The little drops land with a low thud before streaking through the freshly laid charcoal, smearing the shading I had just finished. Blinking a few times and pawing the wetness from my eyes, I finally refocus to realize this drawing is a portrait of Jack. Startled, my hands clasp at my chest. The free-falling liquid from my face has perfectly hit the corners of his eyes, running down the page in his reflective, tear-stained face. His handsome features stir my heart.

When I lean back in my seat to gain a different view, the overall sense of compassion emanating from the image baits more leaking from my eyes. and the shift within me moves again. Ruby and Sorcha are right. Jack would be so mad at me if he knew how I have been wallowing and turning away from all that matters most. It had been a coward move, I know that, but I thought I was doing right by his memory.

Shae pops into my mind, and, without a doubt, there is only one place I want to be right now. I may not be able to have Jack's arms around me ever again, but there is a wonderful man minutes away who wants me just as I am, broken bits and all. Slamming my book closed and packing up in a hurry, I run. Not away from anything, but toward the one thing I can't stand to lose at this moment.

Shae

The light is getting low in the sky as I finally wake up, not realizing I had slept the day away, nor that the exhaustion had run that deep. Hauntings from the past have a way of doing that to you. The hotel room seems barren, cold, and lifeless without her here. Then again, life in general does in her absence. As I shake the hazy sleep from my head, the sound of the hotel key being forced into the lock followed by a rush of eager hands has me quickly up on my elbow as waves of long, blonde hair furiously tumble through the entrance.

Her mismatched eyes catch mine and steal my heart on the spot, rendering me incapable of ever telling her no to anything she desired. The heat flashing in them has me hard instantly; I've come to know that look quite well and strive to do anything I can to keep it there once it surfaces. That single glance undoes me every time. Fuck if I even care about what happened earlier now that I am trapped by the liquid desire exuding from her in this moment. She comes to me in calculated, sultry steps, her thick ass swaying as she nears. Her eyes track my every move, attempting to read my readiness to receive her. *Oh, pet, I am more than ready.* When I throw back the covers as my answer, my erection juts from my hips, tenting my gym shorts as I hold my hand out in invitation.

Taking my hand with caution, she slides along me, igniting my building need. Urgency takes over as I clasp her and pull her rapidly down, unable to stand another minute without her skin touching mine. She lands on top, straddling my hips as she rips off her shirt, and my hands reach up and unclasp her bra, freeing the most gorgeous pair of tits I've ever laid eyes on. They bounce. Like a moth to a flame, I sit as my mouth eagerly seeks a pink, taut nipple.

"Yes!" She moans in an animalistic tone that is music to my ears.

"Fuck, Jade. Bein' away from ye was torture." I groan against her soft flesh, unable to get close enough.

"I'm sorry, Shae." Her hips grind down hard, forcing me to hiss and buck under her. Unable to take it, I flip her over so that I can properly devour her.

"There's nothin' to be sorry for. Hush now. I'm starvin'." My hands begin to peel away her pants and thong in one swoop. I damn near rip them as a few threads pop and hiss under my assault.

With a raging hunger, I clasp under her knees and pull slightly, which perfectly bends her knees, parts her luscious thighs, and lines me up for the heaven just north. I run a finger through the dampening slit, and a low growl starts in my chest as I ease down into her.

"Shae?" Jade breathlessly stops me.

"Hmm?" I try to be respectful and pause, but I am completely distracted. I feel as if I haven't eaten in years. Fuck, I'm starving.

"I was thinking about the other stuff you like to do…" Her voice is shy.

"Ropin'?" I scoff, shocked that it is even tumbling from her lips.

"Yeah."

"What were you thinking exactly?" It's almost impossible to hide my creeping excitement just to combine her in the same thought with my other favorite pastime.

"Can you show me what it is?" Her arms fan out against the sheets.

"Really? What brought that on?" She shut down the last time I attempted to explore the topic more with her.

"I can't fully explain it… something about being bound and finding the beauty and pleasure within it."

"I'll be right back." I thickly swallow as my hands slightly falter. Tis no fodder she speaks. Heading to my luggage with shaking hands, I quickly grab one of my travel ropes. Its soft, white fibers glide across my palm as I finger the release on its bind to unravel its lengths. My inner Dom is filled with trepidation. I stalk back over to the bed, eyeing the goddess lying before me with complete trust and a little uncertainty in her eyes.

"Are ye sure about this?" I ask one more time, praying that she still is.

"Yes, please just be gentle." She bites her lower lip. Her shy, but fierce way about her damn near cuts me open to bleed before her.

"I'd never be anythin' but. Sit on the edge of the bed."

She gingerly begins to scoot, stealing my concentration as she goes. I don't know what I want to do more—say fuck it and bury myself balls' deep in her or spend the evening decking her out in a rope corset so those tits are sitting nice and high for my pleasure, or a combination. *Easy there, big guy. If you get too ahead of yourself, you will scare her off for sure.*

"Interlace your fingers, press yer forearms together, and hold them out in front of ye like so." Tucking the coiled rope under the bulk of my arm, I mimic what I am asking her to do. In a most studious fashion, she complies, watching me in fascination. I pinch the end of the rope, the pads of my fingers pulsing with excitement as they work. I release the length and double it over, my free hand tracing the fibers until it hooks at the loop where the rope now bends in half. Placing the loop right where I want it near her wrists, I turn the paired lengths around once and stop.

"Ye doin' okay?" She nods, seemingly mesmerized. I slowly turn the rope around her forearms as I check it. "Remember, if ye feel any numbness, tinglin', or pain, let me know right away."

"Okay. That's really pretty." She smiles before turning her inquisitive eyes back down to the binding. Pausing every four turns, I cross and loop to form an intricate knot, and then proceed. There is something fulfilling on a visceral level to have a beautiful woman bestow you with this amount of trust as you incapacitate her physical ability to do what comes naturally. Reaching close to her elbows, I tie the ends in a bow and stand back to admire how pretty she looks.

"How are yer fingertips?" I quickly press on them to see the skin slightly blanch before briskly returning to a pink, a telling sign that she has good blood flow.

"Good, no weird feelings." She wiggles her fingers to prove her point.

Her breasts taunt me as they push up and out from the position of her bound arms. Unable to hold back, I heed their call, bending to pop a nipple into my mouth.

"Mhm, fuck, ye are perfection, my love," I murmur around her heavy flesh. Encircling a finger into the loop at the top of her rope work, I raise the knot above her head, her arms forced to follow, causing her back to arch.

"Oh, you are naughty." Her breaths come faster, excited by the change.

"Ye have no idea," I purr and force her back onto the mattress. I have no idea what change has come over her, but who am I to question my luck?

"Now what?"

"Now, I have my way."

"You always have your way." Her voice deepens in lust. It is refreshing that she has a bit of brat in her; it stirs me in a carnal way.

"To an extent." My voice deepens in thought. There are many ways I'd like to have my way, but that too must wait.

"Well, let me up to pee, and then you can show me what other perverse things you have on your mind." She winks at me and moves to try to sit up against the restraints I am holding over her head.

"Mhm, nope." A wicked grin takes over my face as I plot how this is about to go down.

"What the hell do you mean, no?" Her incredulous tone tells me my favorite brat is about to come out and play.

"I mean what I say. No, ye may not head to the loo." Sure, a simple explanation could be given at this point, but I rather wait until her horns come out.

"You've got to be fucking kidding me. Let me use the damn ladies' room, Shae." Her jaw clenches and her cheeks deepen in color.

"Or what?" I can't help but ask.

"Or I will knee you in the balls." Her scowl is quite adorable as it deepens.

"That would certainly ruin the evenin'. That bein' said, I still opt for no."

"Shae…" she grits in warning as her legs being to move. Quickly using my heft, I immobilize her.

"Now, now, love, relax and let me show ye." My palms come down on her thighs to keep them in place as I sink between her legs.

"Shae! This is absurd." her words are strangled as my tongue lashes at her pretty, pink lips. Delving in deep, I suckle at her clit while slipping a finger inside of her. She moans as her back arches and bound hands fall back.

It doesn't take long for her to near the peak, the intensity of her full bladder adding to the building pressure that she is experiencing.

"Shae, it's too much. Please, stop," she mewls almost pitifully. Her decent side wishes me to stop for fear of losing control over her bodily functions.

"I'm not gonna stop. Ride it, sweetheart." I groan in delight before resuming my unrelenting pace. She worries too damn much. Her fears won't come true. Her body begins to tremble, her breathing becoming more erratic as she nears the brink. I hum in approval against her sensitive flesh as my ministrations expand, just enough to send her over.

"Oh God!" She screams in ecstasy as she comes all over my fingers, her body spasming in fits as the waves course through her.

I suck harder on her clit and graze it slightly with my teeth, triggering her pussy to clamp down harder on my fingers as her echoing moans of pleasure hit a new octave, and she rolls into an immediate second orgasm. For the love of God, the sound and feeling of having her come undone by my hand has me rock hard and about to come on the spot. Slowing my eager hands that are desperate to see if I can steal a third release from her, I softly kiss the inside of her thighs as I allow her to breathe. Her bound arms flop forward onto her belly, fingertips reaching for me.

"Do ye have any idea how gorgeous ye are when ye come undone for me?" My voice rumbles with hunger as I stalk up her body, flipping her restrained arms back over her head where they belong. Would she have given me any warning to what she had on her mind, I would have fastened a rope under the bed to bring up and secure that loop at her wrists so that she couldn't move them.

Her hooded eyes catch mine, her hips wiggling, threatening to drive me insane. "That's it, ye minx, turn over," I command and promptly help her roll onto her stomach. Grabbing her by the hips, I yank her back so that her ass is sitting high and pretty, ready for me.

"Shae?" Her question lingers in the air as her discomfort begins to re-register in the wake of her orgasmic haze.

"Ye soon will forget about that all over again." No fucking way is she moving an inch unless it's up and down on my cock. Lining the head up, I slam into her silken depths until the hilt hits and my name is falling feverishly from her lips. Giving her a moment to recover, I painstakingly pull back and do it again. My aggressive side is pushing through, that sadistic bit of me that revels in her coalescing pain and pleasure. Greedily, my hands rake over her backside and grip hard. She gasps and shivers, thrusting her ass backward. Better than a green light. No time like the present. Issuing a quick slap square on her left cheek, I wait for the response.

"Fuck yes," she screams.

Perhaps she is dirtier than I had initially given her credit for. Sprinkling a few more swats across her luscious ass, I enjoy the pinking of her skin. It has my fingers digging deeper into the flesh of her hips and pounding hard. Enough of the games, all I want in this moment is to fuck her so hard that she will be feeling me well into tomorrow every time she moves in the slightest. My animalistic need to penetrate her in every way possible becomes all-consuming as I drive into her, my balls slapping against her ass, fueling my building fire. Unrestrained, raw, and bare before her... she has completely unraveled my carefully constructed exterior, unleashing my beast from the depths it is forced to usually dwell in.

The fire burns in my belly, licking down my thighs, wrapping around my ass as I clench to build pressure there for added sensation. On one last thrust, I fall forward across her back, my teeth baring down into her shoulder, marking her as mine as I erupt within her warm, wet depths, releasing everything that I am. Her mirroring shouts of lust and quivering pussy tells me she is coming, too. Our hips rock together, labored breaths spent as we ride it, bodies and souls fused as one. Truly, for a moment's time, I do not know where I end and she begins. Not wanting to separate but feeling the muscle fatigue setting in, I hold her close and bring us to our sides so that we can recover in our fused state. Once settled in, I pull the release on her arms and slowly pluck at the knots, freeing her. She shucks the fibers off and snuggles deep into me, unable to speak. I, too, have no words for that profound exchange.

Chapter 11

<u>**Jade**</u>

The warm London air hits us as we bustle through Trafalgar Square on our long walk to meet my friends. Giddiness fills my being and my feet don't even touch the ground as we careen through the evening crowds, hand in hand. I've never felt closer to Shae than I have over the last few days. When I step over a puddle, the extension of my leg angers the bruises on my hip that decide to remind me they are there. My free hand gently grazes the area in fond memory, and my belly clenches as a flashback from their creation hits. Shae is a versatile lover; the weeks prior to my introduction to his love of Shibari had been gentle and wonderful. The last few days? Straight primitive fucking on a level I never even knew was possible.

Once I sat in on a psychology class centering around spiritual connections and the topic of soul fucking came up. I honestly can't remember how exactly we shifted onto a subject as explicit as that, but we were discussing the different types of connections we experience with those who cross our paths. Essentially, when two souls recognize each other and connect on a deep level, uncaring of any standards or boundaries, they unionize in the most poetic, unconventional form and fashion a bond that cannot be broken. To soul fuck is to enter into the depths of one another, into the darkest parts, and fuck away all insecurities, self-doubts, fears, etc.... None of that can exist in the light they create. Rules don't apply in this exchange, all bets are off. All that is the melded energy of your two forms come together to create synergistic beauty. There is no separation between the two in that moment. And the experience can simply ruin you.

Essentially, that is what happened between us. Shae channeled our profound connection in a sexual manner that freed me from myself, from my pain, from the guilt and grief that clung to me like a wet blanket. I hate that our time will be coming to an end. At least we have the here and now. Not all good things are meant to last forever, and that is okay. He's given me gifts that will last a lifetime.

"All right, here we are." Shae breaks me from my thoughts as he holds open the door to the noisy pub where we are meeting everyone. I hurriedly rush in, holding Shae tight as I tow him furiously behind me, eager to hug my crazy bunch. Weaving through the pressed bodies, I spy some familiar-looking faces crowded around a high-top table.

"Sorcha," I holler and try to get around, but a large, hulking figure rudely sidesteps to further block my advancement.

"Excuse me, could you please move?" I impatiently huff while tapping him on the shoulder.

"Well, gorgeous, is that any way to great an old friend you ran out on?" James turns around with a huge, shit-eating grin, opening his arms for a hug. Seeing my hand still wrapped around Shae, he drops his arms and begins to size up my guest. Shae, in turn, steps in close behind me, wrapping an arm around my waist and

~178~

releasing my hand. He extends it to formally introduce himself to James.

"Hey, I'm Shae, and ye are?"

"James, Gavin's brother." James lifts a chin toward Gavin, who is now watching closely from his shadowy seat. The others haven't noticed our arrival yet.

"Nice to meet ye. Now, my love, where are the others?" Shae kindly asks, but he clearly dismisses James, unimpressed with his more-than-welcoming initial greeting. James postures slightly before throwing a bit of shade toward Shae and leading the way to the table. Happy squeals sound out as Molly sees us. Sorcha soon follows, trying to get up from the table, but Gavin drapes an arm around her shoulders, keeping her put. Her face turns red in frustration, and she gives me a "help me" look.

I sneak out from Shae's protective hold, running to my lot of misfits and tightly embracing each one of them.

"It's about fuckin' time, princess!" Samuel wraps his long arms around me, giving a mischievous grin to Shae, whose teeth are grinding. After having his moment of fun, he finally eases the building pressure. "You must be Shae. Name's Samuel. This here is my partner, Reed." Shae's shoulders notably relax as he makes their acquaintance. Reed looks as handsome as ever, his darker features strikingly standing out next to Samuel's lighter ones. They are a handsome pair indeed.

"Shae, this is Ben and his husband Steve. This is Molly… and that pair ya already know." I laugh and circle around to give Sorcha the biggest hug I can, though she won't get off the stool, so it makes it hard. Shae animatedly begins chatting with everyone, his good looks and charms easily winning them over as I zero in on Gavin and Sorcha.

"Why are you stool bound?" I pointedly ask.

"I was a clumsy ass. I decided I needed to hurry across a flat faster than I did and tripped and fell."

"Oh God, is everything okay?" Panic floods me.

"Yeah, the vampire is alive and kicking. They think I might have slightly pissed off a disc in my back, but I didn't want any x-rays or anything as the baby is too little yet." Her hand lovingly caresses her small bump. She made it seem like she had gained fifty pounds already, but I doubt she's even put on ten. Well, if she did, it all went to her boobs.

"Jesus, your tits are bigger." I gasp and Gavin proudly smirks before turning his head away at risk of getting smacked by a glaring Sorcha.

"Yes, thank you for noticing. My hips decided to extend as well. One trimester not even complete, mind you."

"I thought the boobs didn't come until later." I snicker.

"Just blessed, I guess." She harrumphs and picks up her water.

"Thank you, Gavin, for taking care of her." I come around and squeeze him tight, so grateful for all that he does. He really is an amazing big brother, in his own quiet… slightly disturbing kind of way.

"He gets the thanks? What about the incubator over here growing your new niece?"

"It's too early to tell if it's a girl," I say, grumbling at her for momentarily getting my hopes up.

"And who's to say the Durham boy streak will end this soon?" James butts in, slamming his beer down on the table and popping on a stool right next to Gavin.

"What streak is that?" I laugh off his attempt to be near me and circle back around to sit next to Sorcha. Shae is still engaged in a deep conversation on who knows what with Samuel, Reed, Ben, and Steve.

"Don't ask," Sorcha says under her breath, and Molly giggles.

"All the Durhams in the last four generations have only ever had sons," Molly proudly fills us in, looking up in time to find James regarding her closely, which has her dropping her chin and blushing. Great. It was no secret that James was a ladies' man, but it's an entirely different thing to see it live and in person.

"Fuck that, it's a girl, and I'm going to see to it that she gives her ole dad just as hard of a time as I do." Sorcha laughs. Her plotting can never lead to any good. Gavin lets everyone get a chuckle in before caressing the nape of her neck with a thick palm, his thumb tracing her soft skin. She relaxes into his touch, her eyes lowering in surrender. I've always thought he balanced her out well, but I never understood that look she gives him until now. As if knowing I needed to feel his presence, Shae shifts to stand behind me, rubbing the small of my back. His breath tickles my neck as he moves to kiss my cheek. I stare adoringly at him, the rest of the room momentarily disappearing, until Molly and Sorcha disrupt the moment.

"Damn it, Jade. Y'all have had weeks together. I want to hear all about your travels," Sorcha demands.

"Oh, yes. Tell us all about the art and food and argh. I don't know what I want to know about first," Molly says.

"We will get to all of that. First, catch me up to what all of you have been up to. Molly, how's Gibson?" I regret asking the minute I do as her face screws up a bit and emotion threatens to take her over.

"That one ended up being a fucker like the rest of them," Sorcha explains for Molly, and then begins in on the upgrades to the house that they've made as well as her art and how it's grown. Molly slowly regains herself as Sorcha does what she does best—talk. She's quite the conversationalist who can charm the toughest of crowds with her candor. That's one of the reasons Daz, her old boss and Gavin's current one, had her schmoozing in the high-roller rooms. After she finishes, Ben and Samuel take their turns, their partners adding in a few cents here and there. Not long after, the whole group is vibing and conversing on a level that reminds me why I am so excited to get back home, immersed in the familiarity waiting there.

"Here ya are, loves." James pops up out of nowhere with a bunch of drinks, pushing a familiar one toward me with a knowing wink before turning his full-watt charm onto Molly.

"Where the hell did you just come from?" I joke as I eye the glass suspiciously. I hadn't even seen him get up.

"I'm everywhere." He laughs before pushing another toward Molly.

"James, if I didn't know any better, I'd say you are trying to get me drunk." Molly scoots closer to him.

"Can't blame a man for trying, gorgeous." He lowers his face to talk to her more intimately.

That's when I happily sip my drink and look around my group of friends as the energetic bar pulsates around us, the live band gearing up on stage. Gavin and Sorcha cuddle up, Molly and James now, Ben and Steve, Samuel and Reed, and Shae and me. Sure, when we head back to San Fran, Molly and I will be back to the single life, but at least for now, we are all happily paired for the evening.

Sorcha, Molly, Ben, Samuel, and I have been friends for years, the group of us weathering many storms. For the longest time, I had been the only one married, getting lots of flak for the choice as the rest of them brought back horror story after horror story about life in the dating world. It hadn't mattered much to me. I had been very happy with my few college experiences leading me straight to Jack, and I never looked back.

As the band blares to life, my heart jumps with the new rhythmic beats, and my feet itch to dance. Leaning into Sorcha, I cup my hand to talk to her. "You evil woman, how'd you know to pick a place with an awesome live band?"

"I know my best friend and the between-the-sheets tango doesn't count as dancing." She wickedly laughs.

"Yeah, but you can't dance." I pout.

"Wanna bet?" She turns to Gavin. "Babe! Momma needs to shake her groove thang," she shouts loud enough for the whole damn place to hear. Gavin rolls his eyes as he slips off his stool in surrender. Sorcha slowly gets up, taking special care not to twist or turn her back, keeping it rod straight. Our table is the last before the stage, so the bump doesn't have to travel far before her beastly man protectively curls himself around her, gently supporting the small of her back as he takes her hand and moves with her. They fit together beautifully. Following their lead, the rest of our table get ups and joins the shoulder-to-shoulder crowd now flowing with the tunes. I'm having such a good time watching everyone that I don't even think to follow.

"Shall we dance?" Shae's lips brush my ear, sending a shiver throughout my body.

"Well, sir, we've only just met, but I suppose so…" I bat my eyes and stand.

"I have a confession, though we be strangers and all, I'm goin' to try and take ye home tonight." He scent overtakes my senses. Suddenly, as much as I want to be with my friends, being alone with Shae becomes more important. I get to romp around London and possibly one other stop with them before we head back to the states. Shae is leaving me a lot sooner.

"I certainly am not going to stop you from trying." I wink and slip into the folds of moving bodies, daring him to come after me. Before I manage to get a quarter of the way in, he snags my wrist and pulls me to him.

"Keep that up and we will be leavin' quickly," he warns.

"Good then." I peck him on the cheek and begin to sway with the music, uncaring of how I might look. I wasn't a terrible dancer, but I wasn't great. Shae keeps up well, his body flowing with mine. Soon, our bodies take on a whole new tone. I am pressed deep into him, and his hips are making promises my intoxicated brain can't say no to. I pull him down to my level so that I can reach his ear.

"Hey hot stuff, how's about you and me get out of here? I've got an itch I need help scratching." I hear myself say it, but don't believe that it just came out of my mouth. I don't talk like that... Who is this woman?

Shae's eyes flare with heat, and something within me bows. Now, I could never do what Sorcha and Gavin do down at their dungeon thing, but I love being his in the privacy of our room. Looking up at him through hooded eyes, I patiently wait to see the response my brashness will earn me.

"Let's go. Now, woman."

I go on my tiptoes to kiss his cheek. "Well, stud, since you asked so nicely," I smart and turn to take off toward the door. I don't get far before I get a smack on the ass and an arm around my waist to slow me down.

"Wow, where do you think you are going?" Sorcha's classic scowl comes into view, threatening my current high. Gavin is hot on her heels, taking us in, a knowing grin now spreading across his dark features. There's no way he could know about the new sexual adventures Shae has been introducing me to, could he? He's not *that* good.

"I've got plans." I try to brush it off and gather my coat.

"The hell you do. I haven't seen you in months!"

"It's been weeks, drama queen, and this is his last night with me. You get me all to your greedy self the rest of the week." I hadn't intended to sound pained about it, but judging by her expression, my façade slipped.

"Can you stay for just a little longer then?" she pushes, wanting to address how I am really feeling, right on the spot.

"Let her go," Gavin intervenes. "It's about time we get my precious cargo to bed."

"All you care about is the baby. Is that all I'm good for?" Sorcha sasses.

"You know damn well I mean you; you are my everything. The baby is just a bonus. But that is nothing I haven't already tried to drill in you. Let's go." And just like that, she's putty in his hands. They, too, are gathering up their things as we all say goodbye. It's not long before we are all on our ways, ready to continue our evening in our own special ways.

∞

"Thank you for coming tonight and playing nice with everyone." I yawn, fully satiated after a few hours of learning just how flexible I am.

"I really had a good time meetin' everyone. Thank ye for includin' me. Damn fine bunch ye have lookin' out after ye." Shae pulls me in closer. "Hey, I want to clear somethin' up, about our wee spat."

"Shae, it's fine. No need to dwell."

"Nah, I really want to explain. Ye've opened up to me in ways I never dreamt. It's my turn. I've never opened to anyone other than my dad and grandad about all this, and even they only know parts."

And just like that, the intimacy between us takes another leap as he wraps himself around me and starts at the beginning, opening up like a rushing waterfall. His time as a child, his wondrous memories of his mother, who sounds like she fell from heaven with her endless love and grace, all the way up until his time on sea. As he speaks and paints the story with details and emotion, I inwardly retreat for a moment to berate myself for never asking sooner. Sure, I'd ask about his likes and dislikes, but never once have I attempted to sink into the depths of his past, and all that makes him who he is. How self-absorbed in one's grief do they need to be to forget such common decencies? Even that is not an acceptable excuse. It's not often we are moved to shift our perspective to a higher level, one that exists outside of ourselves to a picture so crisp and clean, free of emotional baggage and removed from the weight of our own issues, so that we can simply appreciate and be grateful for the true beauty of what is.

From here, many truths are revealed, laid out for my eyes to see. The backstage pass into his temper, his own personal demons, the flip side to the gentleness he's shown me in the face of those he fought for money in the underground rings… it all came to light under the moon streaming into our room through the open window as we lay together in a most vulnerable position. My eyes grow heavy as tales of his mother's cooking flits in through the background. The soft stroking of the warm pads of his fingers across the span of my hips lures me under into the most peaceful sleep I've had in years, one completely free of the nightmares that liked to dance in the periphery, forever shadowing any attempt at peace.

∞

"Jade, my love. Wake up." Shae's voice beckons me from the depths of a heavenly dream.

"What's wrong?" I hazily ask, trying to figure out why he would be waking me up at this hour.

"Come with me onto the porch." I peek up at him from under the pillows to find a robe being held out to me.

"Okay then," I hesitantly reply, slowly rising under the weight of my soreness from his greedy hands.

He takes my hand and pulls me up off the bed before tenderly wrapping me into the robe and leading me out onto the little balcony.

"Shae! It's raining and I'm getting soaked!" I grumble.

"Umm, that would be a correct observation. Now, come here." He pulls me in close, one hand at the small of my back, the other holding my arm in a dancer's position. He begins to sway to a rhythm that isn't audible, but it's beautiful all the same, and my body can't help but follow. As he spins me out in a turn and pulls me back to him, laughter erupts from my depths as my head falls back to feel the drops land on my face. Joy spills freely from my being as he continues to lead us, my love for the rain consuming the moment. In this, pain, heartache, anxiety, depression… none of that can possibly manifest in a pure and glorious moment such as this. His own mirroring laughter adds to the music we are making, a sweet, baritone reverberation seating itself into my soul as it soars. I will never forget this moment or the sound of our combined laughter for as long as I live. It's not every day one gets to dance with an amazing lover on a balcony in London under a refreshing, three AM rain cloud. Fuck, did I just say that to myself? Fear eclipses me as I stuff all those feelings back into a box, put in on the shelf of my vault, and slam the door shut.

Chapter 12

Jade

"I can't believe in just a few hours we have to go our separate ways. Want to come to breakfast with us all before you head out?" I nonchalantly yawn and stretch out as the morning rays hit us through the slight part in the full curtains.

"Ye really think that is a good idea?" My detachment irks him immediately as he shifts away from me.

"Why wouldn't it be?" Confusion pinches my nose as I shift my naked form against the sheets to turn toward his retreating warmth.

"Because..." He trails off, contemplating the obvious elephant in the room, before his voice finds its strength. "Because ye refuse to come to Scotland with me, and partin' will be hard enough. No need to drag it out in front of them." He sighs.

I've got nothing. It's true, I won't agree to that, not when I know this remained temporary fun in my whirlwind, once-in-a-lifetime vacation. Sure, I like him a lot, but let's be honest, this isn't some fairy tale. I am grateful for the time we've had together. It's helped me rediscover a large part of myself that I hadn't realized was missing.

"Jade." He pauses, suddenly shifting his weight over me, leveling his gaze directly with mine as he clasps my hands in one of his, pinning them over my head, making it impossible to move if I wanted to, regardless of our positioning. "My bonnie lass, I love ye with all of my heart." His voice caresses me with a level of emotion I am not quite capable of hearing, and his lips hover just over mine, their heat taunting me.

"Shae, in prior debates over romantic era-inspired pieces, you've clearly stated that you've never been able to fully describe the emotion of love where anyone outside of your family is concerned. How can you possibly know that you love me? I'm damaged goods. We've talked about this." Leave it to me to ruin our first 'I love you' in an awkward, defensive move, trying to protect what little bits are left of my broken heart.

"Are ye always this impossible, woman? Let's get one thing straight first." His eyes glint with a ferocity that had me sucking back my breath. Can't say that I blame him given how I returned the endearment. "Not a damn thing about ye is damaged. Ye are strong. Look, showin' me all of you, good and bad, as well as takin' a chance on us despite it all over the past few weeks, makes ye the strongest person I know. It's been my honor to be gifted with yer vulnerability. Most aren't strong enough to ever do that. Second…" He growls, his jaw tightening, making my entire being feel like an exposed nerve. "I may never be able to contend with yer loss but I fuckin' know when I am in love. But since ye be too damn logical, let me lay it out. Ye know how when ye are blessed to view a perfect sunset that takes yer breath away with no explanation other than its simple existence? That's how I feel every damn time I look at ye, in complete awe and wonderment." He lifts my chin as tears spill down my cheek. "Why won't ye let me love ye?" His tenderness is back with the rasping of his deep voice.

I feel the fear upon my back as I scramble for a response, my emotional side now battling with my logical in an all-out war. "Shae, please, if I dare fall for you in that way, I'll never recover should something go wrong, and I can't ever go through that pain again." I whimper as his forehead pushes against mine in frustration, and a low rumble erupts from his chest.

"I think ye are more ready than you care to admit." Disappointment flashes in his eyes as he eases off me, and the covers all fall back in a whoosh.

"Shae…" My hands reach for him, but he looks upon me like the scorned man he is in this moment, the pain of our reality making his handsome features fall. The further he retreats from me, the smaller our quaint hotel room with vintage charm feels.

"Don't worry about it. I dinnae say all tat with the expectation tat ye'd have a response I'd wanna hear. I'm gonna go for a run before we pack up." His thick accent deepens in emotion to where I struggle to understand against the stinging words now cutting into my soul.

Instead of groveling at his feet, I give the man the space he needs and head to the shower, still stunned by his admission and my crap response. Crouched with my hand under the facet, I deftly crank the knob and stare off into space as I wait for the tired pipes of the cute, but antiquated, English hotel to produce warm enough bathing water.

Shae's deep tone echoes from the bedroom as he mutters to himself in a tongue I don't know as he throws on his gym shorts. I sneak a peek at his glorious, half-naked figure over my shoulder, seeing his large frame bent over to tug on his shoes. He doesn't spare me another glance as he storms out the door, the slamming of wood eliciting a jump from my quaking body. I hadn't realized how cold or shaky I'd become as adrenaline pumps through me. Pulling the squeaky release to start the shower spray, I climb into the tub and sink to the bottom, allowing the water to pummel me. My knees tuck up into my chest as I rock back and forth, the shaking becoming violent as I fall apart, physically and emotionally torn between the cold floor caressing my ass and the steaming hot water raining down. Memories from my childhood flit through the swirling derby that has become my mind, mixing with my college years and everything else leading to present as I ask myself how it all came to this very moment. How can I let a remarkable man like Shae simply walk out of my like, almost insist upon it? What the fuck is wrong with me?

My feelings for him are quite strong. Obviously, if the conflict can drive me to the bottom of a tub, I'm not entirely the cold-hearted bitch I am coming off to be. Am I? No, I'm not, but I've already made my mind up about this. He leaves to go home today, and I will go stay with Sorcha and Gavin at Gavin's flat that he keeps here in London until it is time to return home.

After the last bellow of pain shudders through me, I shove up from the pits of despair. Tired of it all, I quickly rinse and wrap myself in an oversized towel before stomping out into the suite. Unsure of why I am now acting like a hormonal teen, I continually slam things around the room as I attempt to resume a normal routine of getting ready for the day. *Come on, ya fucking emotions, stay in the vault!* I holler at myself. Aimlessly walking around the bedroom, unsure of how to do anything at all, I pass by the desk full of Shae's belongings and see a letter lying open. The handwriting freezes my heart in my chest as recognition hits me like a freight train. My fingers hover over the open page before tracing the edge as the color drains from my face and my heart palpitates in my chest. Reluctantly, my inquisitive nature gets the best of me. I can't help it; I have to know.

To whomever you may be,

Well, this has to be one of the strangest things I've ever done, and I was in a frat in college. So, here I am, writing a letter to another man on behalf of the most important person in the world to me. Funny, how the mind can evolve when faced with mortality. But, enough of that. Here's the deal. She is a very hardheaded pain in the ass. She's feisty, determined to take on the world on her own, and rarely likes to ask for help simply because she's too considerate, always wanting to make life as easy as possible on everyone else around her. She's also an artist, so she is constantly walking in two worlds, reality and wherever else she goes in that brilliant but slightly mad mind of hers... and that means she forgets simple things like closing cabinet doors, paying bills, and putting things away. Actually, you might just want to hire a maid. She's a terrible housekeeper, choosing to get lost in that creative space in time rather than do basic things. Hold on, I know what you probably are thinking, but I am not a complete dickhead. It is all of that, and so much more, that makes her more precious than anything else on this earth. I am sure by now you've gathered an opinion on that ever-

working mind of hers. The damn thing never shuts off, I promise. I am pretty sure she even holds debates with herself while sleeping that would give the best presidential nominees a run for their money based on her dream-state mumblings I've listened to for years. But it is just as dazzling as her beauty. She is the total package. She is the reason the sun rises every morning, why birds will hover just a little nearer to sing when she's with you, and why life in general is sweeter in her presence. I have never met another person who loves as passionately, walks as lightly or purposefully through life, and who cooks green chili that tastes like it fell from heaven. Damn it, you lucky bastard, I wish I could take her chili with me.

Anyway, I know that if you are reading this, cancer won. Don't go crying me a river about it; I've found a strange peace around it that I can't quite explain. Once upon a time, I saw this natural doctor when treatment first started to explore my options. He gave me some tips, as well as went out of his way to let me know that death, in its own way, was a form of medicine. Now, let me tell you, at the time, I flipped my lid, not ready to hear it. But now? After almost a year of pure hell? I welcome it. Sure, this was not how I planned on living my life, and God is the only one who knows the whys behind my suffering and the true purpose of all this. I believe there is one, a purpose. I just don't fucking know for what.

Since I am talking to you about all this shit, it also means she was brave enough to open her heart to another, and Gavin, that junkyard dog, agrees you aren't half bad. We know you won't ever compare to the likes of my skinny ass, but you must be something special, too. Seriously, though, all joking aside, please, I ask you with everything I've got left in my corpse of a body, take care of her. She will fight you every step of the way, but don't let that stop you. As for me, she needs to let me go. I, Jack, am giving you both permission to please fucking let me go. Be guilt free as you find comfort in each other's arms. I really am at peace with it. Someone as perfect as she is needs to be experiencing life to the absolute max, including being loved, not wallowing. I made her promise to go on living. And she'd never intentionally break a promise to anyone. My fear, however, is she may unintentionally do it, lost in that mind of hers. Be patient and help her get there. She deserves it all, and we both know she is worth it.

Now, a few things she'll never tell you. She hates red roses, calla lilies, and those yellow roses with orange tips are the motherlode. She forgets to eat, constantly, and gives a whole new meaning to the phrase "hangry". Keep her fed and tanked on coffee. She loves the ocean... It's as if it's actually a part of her. Never let her move far from it; that'd be as good as clipping her wings and throwing her in a cage. Now, this is some downright gold I am giving you. I expect some of her next batch of fall chili on my headstone for this. When it rains, take her hand, pull her out into it, and dance with her. Just trust me. And lastly... well, there's so much more, but I am trying to keep it short and sweet. I just want to say thank you. Thank you for coming into her life and taking care of her. I owe you big.

~Jack

P.S.

Jade, I know you will read this after whoever else does, because you are nosey like that. I love you, baby. Thank you for the best years of my life, no matter how short they may have been. In reality, forever would never have been long enough. But it really is

~195~

time for you to let go of me and fall freely into the present. Love without limits, break all boundaries, and let that wondrous lust for life you have to take the lead. Don't ever dull yourself for the sake of my memory, for if you do, I will have to come back and haunt your stubborn ass. And I am talking Poltergeist style, none of that Ghost type stuff.

The letter falls from my trembling hand back onto the woodgrain of the desk. I feel as if I'm suddenly a naughty child caught with my hand in a cookie jar. This is a private letter that my dead husband wrote to my future lover, and somehow, the universe conspired for Shae to be the recipient. And I've been scolded in a number of ways for trespassing on the secrecy, as well as not opening up to the one man I should. Hell, even Jack is fucking rooting for the man. How the hell did Shae get this? As soon as I ask myself the question, the answer hits me square in the jaw, Gavin. That's right. He mentioned Gavin in the letter. My big brother from another mother is also trying to tell me to not be so stupid. He conveniently handed this over their first night in London, in hopes I wouldn't walk away.

I'm standing in the middle of a crossroads, not sure whether to go left or go right. To get angry or give in to the emotions beckoning me to give in already and fall for the man. *Jack, you sonofabitch. How dare you, how dare you conceive of giving me away to another before you had even passed. Sure, you were doing it out of love and compassion, but I didn't need your sympathy then, and I don't need it now.*

And while I am at it, is that the reason Shae woke me up before dawn to dance in the rain? Because my dead husband told him to and he wanted to see if it was true? And why the fuck did Jack have to be such a big person about it all when I can barely leave the infantile state I constantly regress to in the wake of his memory? Feeling violated and exposed in ways I refuse to deal with, and allowing anger to win, I decide it's time to make a break for it.

The room spins as I rush to throw on my clothes, comb my hair, and pack up every little bit of my belongings, shoving them all into whatever pocket or slot I can find. Every time my fingers come across something that is Shae's, I tremble and backslide momentarily before resuming my speed. Goodbyes are hard enough. I hate them, always have. I'll be damned if I cry another tear over any man, ever again. Feeling spiteful and fully in the moment of my regression, I reach in into the fold of my suitcase and grab the first soft thing I come into contact with. The silk panties I pull out seem quite appropriate. That's all this was, right? Sex? Laying them out on the desk, I scribble a note to go with them and head out the door. Fuck this, fuck him, and fuck Jack for that matter.

Chapter 13

Shae

Sitting on the tarmac, awaiting my flight to take off back to Scotland, I sit in a stunned state. She fucking up and left me, like I was nothing, like our time together meant absolutely nothing. My clenched hand hasn't let up on the panties or note she left me, which are now stuffed together in my pocket. The scrawled words keep playing over and over in my head.

Dear Shae,

Thank you for everything, but let's be real. All it ever was going to be was a good time. I found the letter from Jack. I can't help but feel a bit used and conspired against. Perhaps that is all we were doing, using each other... or maybe it's all just my own issues winning out. Who knows? I wish you the best.

~ Jade

Was the woman that bloody cold? I sure as hell didn't see that coming at all. Did our time really mean nothing to her? It fucking meant everything to me. The rational part of me tries to understand the pained place where she might be coming from, but my bruised ego chimes in and says fuck it. If she can't realize what she ran away from, who am I to try and make her see? I've work to do, a family back home itching to see me, and a life waiting for me to embrace it.

I may never understand her callousness, nor do I ever really want to. She rightly warned me from the beginning, but being the Dom I am, I thought I could break down her walls and find my way into her heart. Well, the joke is properly on me. She crawled into mine, making me drunk on my feelings before daggering it to hell and leaving. Fantastic.

Jade

"Let me be the one to save Sorcha from always having to be the bitch. You're an idiot," Samuel states, and Ben and Molly nod in agreement.

"Well, isn't this a delightful brunch?" I snap and guzzle my Bellini, wishing the background sounds of the packed restaurant would drown them all out.

"Hey, sister, we're your friends, not your paid ass kissers," Samuel bites back before his dimples deepen in amusement.

"You get the truth, always," Molly adds.

"Yeah, whether I want it or not. I told all of you just like I told him, my heart will never be given away to another again. I refuse to risk being in that kind of pain again." I huff and tuck the same strand of hair behind my ear that won't seem to stay back.

"And you are just fooling yourself. Ya already gave it to him the minute you submitted," Sorcha says, pleased with herself.

"How do you know that?" I challenge, suddenly very uncomfortable in the face of having my intimate life open for discussion.

"Honey, please, do you know who your audience is? We are all in the lifestyle, even if your rope burns weren't enough of a sign." They all snicker at that, watching me closely as they dive back into their food to give me time to process.

"Welcome aboard." Gavin raises his glass to me with a wink.

"Fuck off, all of you," I mumble, rather bitterly, and go back to ignoring them as I stare at my full plate of greasy food. It tastes like crap, and my appetite has fled.

"Someone is having a bad subdrop." Reed chuckles, earning him a reprimanding scowl from Samuel. Quickly dropping his eyes back to the table, Reed avoids the subject further. Molly, Steve, and Sorcha, who all identify more with the sub role, equally fall quiet from the exchange even though Samuel didn't even say anything.

"What's a subdrop?" I ask Gavin. He's been busy stuffing his face, but now looks up in surprise.

"That emotional drop or extreme shift after intense… interactions with your partner. Usually happens when the adrenaline and endorphin release is substantial," Gavin explains through mouthfuls, cautious of the passersby.

"Oh." I sit with that for a few, the term appropriately fitting for our last evening together as well as the emotional flare this morning.

Gavin's phone begins to buzz. Sorcha shoots it the death glare as he apologetically looks to us and excuses himself.

"Fucking Daz," Sorcha mutters.

"Doesn't he know you are on vacation?" Steve asks.

"Please, that pompous ass doesn't care. He wants his errand boy at his beck and call."

"And let's be honest, Daz needs to get laid," Samuel adds, pointing the tip of his fork at the phone.

"He's the owner of all those clubs and can't get laid?" Astonishment colors my tone. The man isn't hurting financially and carries himself with an air that has women fanning themselves on the rare occasion he surfaces from the shadows. Out of the corner of my eye, I see Molly shift uncomfortably in her seat and send her attention to somewhere else in the restaurant.

"He can get laid any time he wants. It doesn't mean he does. No man truly wants what's easy. We are hunters, baby. We need to feel like we worked for it for us to really appreciate our kills." Samuel gives me one of those looks that curls my toes and makes my heart beat a tad faster. He may hate vajay, but that doesn't mean he can't command a desired response when he wants to. Ass.

"Well, moving on. What are we up to today?" Molly interjects, nervously pushing up the sleeves on her blouse, clearly in a hurry to change the subject. Sorcha's assessing eyes start to dissect her instantly, but she stays quiet.

"How about we string ya along to some of the top monuments?" Samuel pushes, his implications not lost on me.

"Ha. Ha. Is this how it's gonna be? Rope joke after rope joke? How the hell do you even know exactly what I got into?"

"Yes, Miss 'I'm going to find a way out of every club mixer', you are most definitely going to be hearing quite a bit of it." Ben laughs as Steve leans into him, resting his head on his shoulder.

"And, in answer to your question… I saw him around the club a few times when he was working in the city. He helped me perfect a few restraining techniques I was trying to nail down." Reed shivers slightly next to Samuel, but doesn't say anything. "When I met him last night, and saw your wrists, it all fell into place." Samuel proudly reveals his sleuthing skills.

"Glad to know I've been the topic of your gossip." I hate my personal business being out for discussion. It is one thing to sit one on one with any of them, but as a group, it made me uncomfortable.

"Oh, stop it. You were fucking glowing. It was like my old childhood friend was back and better than ever. Now you are back to your grumpy, prematurely aging self," Sorcha scoffs.

I chuck a grape at her and resume my pissed-off state. "Where's James?" I ask Molly as I stifle a smartass snort, my intentions not all pure as I dig for information in my insecure state.

"Don't know," Molly deflects, not wanting to talk about it.

"Yeah, sure ya don't." Samuel's rich laugh ebbs.

"He scooted out of her hotel room before the sun came up." Ben laughs, and Steve elbows him.

"He did not!" Molly tightly crosses her arms. "I know he's a ladies' man. Y'all don't need to remind me. It's about all I've been able to attract. But rest assured, I didn't fall for it this time."

"So, what's his name?" Sorcha prods, and everyone else zeros in on Molly. Happy to have the attention off me, I grab the only thing I can think to stomach on the table, drain it, and motion for the waitress to top off my Bellini.

"I don't know what you are talking about."

"Wow, stupid move." I laugh.

"The geek fucked up, and ya dumped him faster than Sorcha would a one-night stand. Can't say I blame ya. That dude was a douche. But what gives?" Samuel asks.

"Samuel, you have the facts all wrong. The geek broke the foundational rules in their contract. She rightly ended their arrangement. Then she takes a break from the club, finally comes back, and disappears into a private room for the night, only to resurface and hasn't been back since. She hasn't slipped and fallen on any D since either. Now, our bubbly cheerleader is suddenly defensive over whether she did or did not sleep with a man whore." Sorcha's sarcastic tone would feel like a biting whip to some, but she really is just that analytical. She is the most supportive and nonjudgmental person I've ever met. Her intentions are always in the best interest of others, thank god. If her heart were black, she'd be capable of doing some serious damage.

I choke on my Bellini when she calls James out for being a whore. Diving for my napkin, I chase the sputtering flecks off my face.

"Ah shit, you fucked the man whore too? Nice job, way to dust the cobwebs off." Samuel grins from ear to ear.

"Can anyone have a scrap of privacy with you all?" My cheeks blaze.

"He's pretty hot. Can't blame ya, sister," Ben adds.

"Yeah, and he's got big feet." Steve chuckles, turning up the red factor of my face a few more degrees.

"You all are impossible. Why don't we get back to Molly?" I shoot her an apologetic look as she glares at me.

"I'm not talking anymore about it." She puts her hands up in surrender as her red curls bounce back and forth.

"Well, we can always sit here and pick apart facts and draw our own conclusions. Steve and I happened to be at the club that night," Ben jokingly threatens, brushing back his long, brown hair, causing Molly to sink in her seat further, her grey eyes widening in fear.

"It's nothing to be concerning yourselves with. It's probably nothing I should be concerning myself with for that matter." Her bottom lip quivers in frustration lines her face.

"What did I miss?" Gavin asks as he sits back down, his heavy palm immediately seeking Sorcha's thigh. Her hand automatically rises to stroke the back of his neck, giving him a comfort only she knows he needs in that moment. She really can tame the beast unlike anyone else. James had even made a comment about how he'd rather visit his brother only when Sorcha was around.

"Oh, this little one doesn't want to discuss her latest indiscretions with a mystery man." Samuel nods to Molly. Gavin shoots him a warning glare. Samuel's eyes widen in a wordless exchange, something only I seem to have caught as I glance around.

"Babe, she really isn't comfortable crossing that line." Reed finally finds his voice, sticking up for the redhead on trial.

Samuel smiles adoringly at Reed. "All right, I'll let it go."

"Can we do the double-decker bus tour today?" Reed asks, giving Molly a look of compassion as he diverts the heavy-handed Dom who's been hard on her trail. But I am pretty sure Gavin was the one to end that hunt.

"Oh, that sounds fun, and how about the London Dungeon?" Steve winks, and Sorcha giggles.

"Tourist traps?" I sigh, wanting to explore the British Museum again. They really did have the best exhibit on Egypt that I have seen yet.

"Jade, we are not spending this week touring every museum imaginable within a hundred-mile radius of the city," Sorcha mocks.

"Hey, what's wrong with that?"

"Even I, as a fellow artist, don't want to bore the group on that level."

My heart sinks. I've been quite spoiled the last few weeks, trekking around with a man who loved doing just that.

"Now you've gone and made her sad," Reed scolds, and Steve places an arm over my shoulder.

"It's nothing. We'll do whatever you all want." I pick up my drink, determined I will be drunk by noon.

"That's enough, Jade." Gavin grabs my glass, downs it himself, and sets it down with a final thump onto the table.

My mouth opens to challenge him, I don't care who he thinks he is... but I snap it shut when he levels that scary gaze at me.

"You can't drink him away, hun," Steve softly adds.

"I don't know what you are talking about."

Everyone sighs in unison.

"Seriously, did Gavin tell you how they all conspired against me? With a certain letter?"

Gavin's forehead wrinkles, but he keeps quiet, his whiskey eyes waiting to see how this is going to play out.

"What letter?" Sorcha hesitantly asks her mate, who refuses to respond.

I whip the damn thing out of my purse and drop it on the table for them to all take turns reading. Which is precisely what they do as I try to stomach a fried piece of flesh that might be bacon. After a while, I dare look up. All eyes are on me, their tender stares making me regret the decision to share.

"Jade, babe, that's the sweetest, most selfless thing I've ever read." Molly reaches across the table for my hand, her bangle bracelets alerting me to the advancement. I retract it immediately.

"No, Jack quit on me, conspired with this one," I swing a thumb toward Gavin on my left, "to tell a bunch of private things to a man I am not so sure should have received them, then he, in turn, took advantage and woke me up at three o'clock this morning to dance with me in the rain, using the letter as a how-to without even telling me." Even as I say it aloud, it all sounds stupid and full of the real issue—my fear. My head collapses into my hands in frustration.

"And there she goes, realizing how stupid she sounded." Sorcha gets up, comes around Gavin, and bends to take me in her arms. Her hissing in pain has Gavin guiding her ass to his jean-cladded lap immediately so that she can perch there while holding me. "Let me guess—you prematurely ran him off this morning, too."

I nod into my hands as the tears slowly fall for the world to see. "I'm such an idiot."

"No, for fuck's sake, stop speaking so ill of yourself. You were emotional and not thinking clearly because it shocked you. We all do and say stupid shit when we are backed into a corner we didn't see coming. Just ask this one." She turns and pecks Gavin on the cheek.

"I'm sure if you just explained yourself, he'd understand," Ben adds.

"Nope, pretty sure leaving him a 'thanks for the good time as that is all that it was' note and walking out without a goodbye was enough to make him hate me."

Samuel shakes his head, but, for once, keeps his mouth shut as Reed's eyes grow larger.

"First of all, you know that Jack didn't quit on you, right?" Molly gets back to the basics, our ever-present counselor.

"Yes, Molly, I see that now I've had a minute to cool off."

"Second, he was just trying to do something to make you happy. He wasn't trying to use the information he was provided to manipulate you." Molly insists.

"Yeah, he's not that type, I know."

"And I only gave him the letter last night after seeing the two of you together. I knew he was the one it was meant for," Gavin finally defends himself.

"Jack really entrusted you with that?" I didn't doubt the choice, more so that Jack would actually do something like that.

"Shocking, I know, but I have a gift of reading people." Gavin smirks, knowing I didn't mean offense.

Sorcha's flowy top shifts across her man as she stands, unable to sit in that uncomfortable position any more.

"It's too late. He's already caught his flight back to Scotland, and I feel like I need to give him space after the last few days. He wanted me to come with him."

"And you said no?" Steve asks in disbelief.

"Yes I did. It's never going anywhere. I may feel bad for acting like a child, but that doesn't change the fact that I have a life to get back to and so does he.

"The man drops his life for how many weeks to jet set with you, and you couldn't go home with him for even a week? Shit, you could go two weeks and still have plenty of time to get ready for classes." Sorcha levels her incredulous gaze at me.

"To do what? Prolong the inevitable? He lives a sea away, and I have no desire to give my heart fully to anyone ever again. Can't y'all just respect that? It was fun while it lasted. I'll find a way to apologize for being a bitch. He deserves that at least."

Reed and Steve, the two eternal romantics of the group, hang their heads as Molly's psychobabble begins to brew in her head as she assesses how to address my obvious denial. Ben, Gavin, and Samuel, the big, bad Doms, all shift intensely.

"Fuck, sister, you are an emotional masochist." Sorcha shakes her head and finds her seat on the other side of Gavin.

"Seriously? You are one to talk. And Samuel—" I shoot him a warning as I see him opening his mouth; he can be just as bad as Sorcha. "Don't even try either; you are just as bad as that one. You know what? Have a good day, everyone. Maybe I will see you for dinner... I'll let you know." I get up, throw some currency on the table for my portion, and walk out on them all.

Who needs this crap? In the past, I would have stuck around and taken the verbal bashing, afraid to venture out on my own or set a boundary when they crossed a line. But traveling the world and having a beautiful man break you out of your confines has a way of putting a new set of brass balls on you. It's my choice who I do and do not invite into my life for the long term. I don't want long term with anyone ever again. So what if I care deeply for the man? How could I not? He came into my life at a time that I needed him most and taught me more about myself than I ever knew possible. We made beautiful memories together that I will cherish for the rest of my life. Sure, he weaseled his way into my heart in a certain capacity, but the love that grew there was no more than what I have for any of those knuckleheads now watching me through the window as I head back to the flat.

Rounding the block, I pass by a little café I hadn't seen on the way there. The heaviness in my heart lifts a bit as I decide to head in and find my zen. It's not long before I am seated at a little table, a steaming mocha in hand as my eyes glaze over my spread-out notebook in thought. My fingers find their way to the pages, sifting through the sketches I felt inspired to do in Paris, the first real connection I had with art on a personal level since Jack died. I'd squeaked out about a dozen. I hadn't realized there were so many.

As the pages turns, the woman entrenched in vines gives me pause as I take her in once more. Her creation on paper stimulated me to break through into who I feel like I am now. Some say people never change, but they are full of shit. People do change, sometimes for the worse, and sometimes for the better. I'm not quite sure where

I fall on that spectrum, but I do know that I am not the same free spirit who enchanted Jack. That's a good thing, though. Jade in college was starry eyed and wore rose-colored glasses. Jade in present day is scarred and a bit jaded, but she still has that sense of adventure and passion. It's just an evolved version now, a realist edition that isn't going to be afraid to ask for what she wants or be true to herself. She's been hurt, knocked down, bloodied a bit, but she's gotten back up. Sure, she may not have done it very gracefully, and inflicted a bit of pain on someone who didn't deserve it... Hell, she's a bit reckless these days. But I fucking love her.

My hand picks up a pencil as tears of revelation percolate. I've never thought about self-love, always assumed it was there, but took it for granted. But you know what? I love every little thing about myself, imperfections and all. I'm pretty fucking amazing. God, that feels good to say! Never have I felt this way about myself. Do I dare say I've been taking myself for granted all of these years? That could very well be the truth. As my hands work the charcoal into what they see fit, my mind lifts to that disconnected happy place. Transcending into that creative heaven, I can't help but send a silent prayer of thanks to Shae. He helped me get to this magnificent moment, and I will find a way to make things right with him someday.

Chapter 14

<u>Shae</u>

"Sir, your three o'clock is here." My assistant's voice chimes over the receiver, ripping me from a daydream. Well, it wasn't a dream, not really; it had been reality not that long ago. Her thick, tan legs bound together as I laved her nipples until she almost came on the spot from that minimal stimulation... The strategically placed knots around her torso and between her legs had helped as well. *Fuck me!* I inwardly groan.

"All right, send them in please." I quickly adjust my hard-on that is attempting to bust through my pants, shifting my high-backed chair to align with my desk. The door to my office opens. A long-legged, bleached blonde now struts her way toward me with purpose. She is finely dressed in a well-tailored suit that hugs her generous curves quite well. Interesting turn of events considering the devious path my thoughts are running down at the moment.

"Mr. MacCain? I am Vivian, the project manager on the Smith renovation." She leans over my desk, flashing me her low-cut blouse, offering her hand in formal greeting. My hungry side wants to turn the charm on, but her presumptuous nature pisses me off. Ignoring the proper thing, which would be to stand and return her introductions, I lean back in my chair, the leather protesting under my shifting weight.

"Sit down, please." I wave dismissively at the seat next to her arched figure. She raises a brow, and her lips form a pinched heart as she retracts her hand, casting me a questioning glance before bringing her ass around to meet the seat.

"Lovely office you have here. Is this mahogany?" She attempts to continue to bait me as her hand strokes the grain of my hand-carved masterpiece with nautical embellishments. It is a showstopper, most definitely. It weighs a ton as well. My granddad and I custom built it, and my dad helped refinish it. I was the first in our family to graduate from a university. The three of us celebrated by constructing the desk I would meet clients from.

"How can I help you?" I cut to the chase, narrowing my eyes, not wanting to mediate pleasantries another minute longer.

Her voice falters as she begins to drone on about the current project that her bosses insist on finding issues with that are, in reality, nonexistent. As her full, pink lips formulate words, my wily side tempts me once more. I could use a good fuck, and she'd be an easy one. My cock kicks in my trousers at the thought of some well-deserved attention. After weeks of constant sex with an insatiable woman, the last few weeks of nothing but a one-handed salute have been miserable. This one is not very bright, but she has an ample ass… Perhaps I can gag her and bend her over this desk so she can get a closer view of the wood as I go balls' deep. My inner beast roars at the thought. Clasping my hands in front of me to appear intrigued by her ramblings, I trace my bottom lip with my index finger as I picture what her bare ass will look like with my cock buried deep. The fake blonde keeps talking about issue after issue, encouraged to keep going by my apathetic murmurings of understanding, and completely blind to the hunger now building in me. Vivian chuckles about something or another. I hear it, but that is not the sound that registers in my ears.

Visions of dancing with Jade suddenly swarm me as the sound of her angelic laugh rings loud and clear. It was the purest, most genuine laugh I had ever heard in my life. Jack, the old dog, hadn't been leading me out onto a ledge at all with his letter. To dance with her in the rain and be a part of the joy it brought her was to sip the very essence of life itself. Her long, beach-blonde waves spin out in front of my vision, the ringlets catching sparkling drops in their clutches as they fall from the sky. It's as if I am turning her this very second, bringing her back to press into my body, her mismatched eyes mesmerizing me as they render me daft, seeing straight into the most vulnerable parts of my soul and loving them as vividly as she did every waking moment she gets to experience.

"Does that sound like a suitable resolution, Mr. MacCain?" The woman's voice calls me from the daydream, disrupting my pleasurable reminiscence, sending a spike of fury throughout my being.

"Let me get this straight. They think it would be a suitable consolation prize to call in another architect to takeover where I have left off, assume my drawings for the foundational reconstruction, and pay me considerably less than my contracted fee? Did I miss anythin'?" My anger becomes palpable. Sure, I hadn't really been listening, caught in daydreams once more, but I sure as hell picked up on the main pieces concerning my project. The same project that lured me back home weeks before I was ready to end my holiday with the fucking love of my life all over Europe.

"Ye-yes, that is correct." Viv-whoever confirms.

My hand comes down on the flat surface before me, the boom thundering throughout the office. "Miss... whatever ye said yer name is, it's not important really, ye can tell yer bosses to go fuck themselves. We have a contract. If they desire to contest it in order to cut funds they just now are realizin' they didn't have, they can take it up with my lawyers. I'm certain ye are smart enough to see yerself out as well. Good day." With that, I shove up from my desk, rising to my full height, and take pleasure in the unease her face now holds, as well as that tinge of a wee bit of lust. My inner asshole can't help it in my messed-up state. Dipping my head in regards, I glower and exit the room, needing to be as far from this place as possible.

My assistant fumbles and calls after me as I storm off, trying to smooth out the mess left in the wake, God bless the woman, but I just don't give a fuck. What I need, right now, is to get my head on straight and jump back in the game to close a few other deals that could potentially take me to various other parts of the world, free from that blasted woman's haunting. Her memory taints every damn thing I do. As I near the exit door from my office, I slam the heavy steel open with a deafening sound as my wingtip dress shoes hit the pavement.

I haven't heard hide or hair from that fucking temptress who ran out on me. It's been two fucking weeks. I've gone round and round in my head on what went wrong or what I could have done differently, but I came up blank. Perhaps I was too engrossed in what I thought was going on between us to see the obvious signs that stared me in the face. Lost in the turbulent wake of the one I can't forget, I let my feet carry me to my car. It's not long before I am hitting the speed limits, rushing toward the one place I know I can go to clear my congested head.

Before long, I've flown the almost two-hour drive from Glasgow to Crail. I pull up to the quaint cottage by the sea that I haven't visited since right before Prague, and throw open the car door. Gratitude fills me as the blast of ocean air hits me hard, chasing away all self-doubt and fear that has been riddling my brain.

"Shae? Is tat my boy?" the old man asks from the porch, squinting against the descending sun at my back.

"Hey, old man!" I holler back, knowing he's got barnacles growing in his ears by now.

"Come! Come!" He ushers me in as the wind begins to pick up, whistling through as it sends its biting chill.

The heat radiates around us as we have a cuppa around the hearth, and I divulge my tale of heartache to my grandad. As I end the story with my arrival, we both sit and stare into the fire in silence. It's a good while before he speaks; he never was one to fly off at the mouth without giving his words a good thinking through first.

"So, wut are ye still doin' here?" he asks, his bushy brow punctuating the question as he picks up his pipe from the end table to stuff it.

"Tryin' to get back to my life." I don't understand where the old man is going.

"Son, ye be just as stubborn as this woman." He sighs and strikes a match. The hiss and pop brings back childhood memories as it touches down into the bowl, clouds of sweet tobacco billowing up in answer to the fire's call.

I rock my chair and pointedly ignore him.

"Ye ain't gettin' any younger, my boy. And ye've ne'er brought a lass home for me to torture either." His wrinkles deepen in humor.

"I'm glad ye find my life so amusin'." It's true, I've dated, but there was never anyone special enough to meet my family.

"Nah, well, a bit perhaps. But I wud like ta see a few wee ones runnin' around here again before I die."

"Funny old man. She does live a sea away."

"Tat's wut ships were made for, or have ye forgotten?" He puffs on his old pipe again, leveling a steady eye my way.

"I thought ye always said no woman was worth crossin' a sea for." I laugh, recalling his drunken rants.

"No average woman, nah. But one tat makes ye want ta be a better man? Aye, tat one ye do."

"But she upped—"

He cuts me off with one look. "Wut? She upped and wut, boy? Was bein' a woman? Should I knit ye a dress now, too?" He blows out a cloud of smoke, and thoughtfully sets the pipe on its tray. "Ye don't net a wild woman, put a bow on her, throw her in the kitchen, and then expect supper ta be ready when ye land. Ye let her run, feck, ye run with her, but ne'er let her run away. Tis the wild ones tat men crossed seas for and fought wars over."

"Ye are a crazy ole nut." I laugh, trying to make sense of what he is getting on about now.

"Perhaps, but I know. I married one." He smiles fondly as he fingers his wedding band.

I've tried not to think too much about my grandmother in the last few years. Her passing devastated me. It followed too close on the heels of my mum's passing. I try not to think about either of them. As I sit here and rock by the fire, the similarities between all the strong women I've admired and loved align. My mum, grandmother, and Jade, a holy trinity if you will. For the love of God, the old coot was right. I never should have let her scare tactic work. I shouldn't have let her push me away. As the lightbulb goes off over my head, I look to the wise old man and get a knowing grin in return.

"Well, wut are ye waitin' for? Go get her and brin' her back for me to show all of yer embarrassin' nappy photos." He chuckles once more as I get up and hug him hard before grabbing my keys off the sideboard.

"I'll call ye later, old man."

Jade

"Sorcha, I don't need to go to the damn doctor," I whine, sounding almost as bad as she normally does.

"Yes, you stubborn mule, you do. You look like hell. I don't know if you picked up a virus or just need an antidepressant, but I'm too fucking pregnant to be worrying after you another minute." She throws my sweater at me and slips her feet into her boots.

"I'll just go back to your apartment and crash. I'll be better in a few days." I tuck my head back under the fleece throw on the couch and curl in on myself as another wave of chills washes over me.

"The fuck you are. Don't make me call Samuel," she threatens. She tosses her long, auburn hair out of her face, her green eyes daring me.

"Oh, what, you don't want Gavin to get sick?" I tease. He's normally her first threat.

"Nah, you wench. He's off on a mission for Daz, the ass. I don't want to stress him out further. I want to get you checked out, then back to my apartment, so I can come back and make my man a proper dinner. Now, scoot!" She comes over and brings her hand down hard on my ass, smacking it with deceptive force, the sting radiating up my aching body.

"Owe!" I scream and jump up, ready to comply rather than be beat by the fiery little Irish woman.

"Don't act like you didn't like it." She laughs and grabs her purse, holding open the door for me. As I make my way toward her, I catch an eyeful of the beautiful masterpiece adorning most of the wall in the dining room, the one with Gavin's picture set in the middle of the interlocking patterns. It remains a testament to their love, and her ridiculous talent as an artist.

I watch the cityscape pass by as we drive, the call of the sea wafting in through the cracked window. The thought of going back home to the apartment by myself makes me sad. Gavin and Sorcha are probably getting tired of me taking up space in their house, though. Maybe I should just get a dog or a cat... perhaps two.

"Have you called him yet?" Sorcha breaks my chain of depressive thoughts, throwing a glance my way before returning it back to the road.

"No, Mom, I haven't." I need to; I really do.

"You need to." She echoes my thoughts and pops a sucker into her mouth, still battling her morning sickness. It's followed her into the second trimester—morning, noon, and night.

"I know! I want to clear the air, but I haven't been able to find the words. 'I'm sorry' doesn't seem like enough. 'I'm sorry I was such a self-centered bitch who shoved off all meaning of our time together, and then chalked it up to a pair of panties, insinuating we had been using each other all along for sex... right after you professed your love' seems a little better, but I think it needs work." I sigh as my body flushes, feeling as if it is trying to get a fever. Lowering my seat back, I curl into the cool leather of the Acura as she pulls into a parking lot.

"Well, let's work on cleaning that up then... right after we head inside." She puts the car in park and releases her seatbelt.

I groan loudly like a petulant child before following her lead. I hate doctors, and I have told her multiple times that the only reason I stayed friends with her is because she dropped out of med school. The true hatred, however, didn't come until Jack's ordeal. After heading in, signing forms, being led back into a sterile room that holds as much welcoming warmth and emotion as drying paint, the staff proceeds to poke, prod, and make me pee in a damn cup. Once the humiliating acts cease, Sorcha and I find ourselves waiting for the doctor to arrive... who is rather late. As I am about to say to hell with it and leave, a mousy woman in her fifties scuttles into the room in a fit of apologies, making me immediately feel bad for my foul attitude about the whole experience.

"All right, Mrs. Ritter, let's have a look at you." She proceeds to examine me further while asking a million questions before taking a chair right across from me.

"Well, Doc, am I going to live?" I joke.

"All signs point to yes." She shuffles some paperwork, bringing one sheet almost clear to her nose. "We took a bunch of blood and urine, it seems. While some had to be sent off to the lab, we were able to obtain a few results here in the clinic. Interesting indeed." She speaks more to herself, leaving me hanging. I feel my heart drop to the linoleum as I wait for answers. "It would appear that, on top of having a bad virus, you are pregnant."

"Excuse me, I'm what?" My hearing radio dials in and out as Sorcha joins the conversation, badgering the doctor with questions about who knows what.

"You are pregnant." That's what I thought she said. And then the world turns black.

"Shhh, she's waking up." Sorcha's worried voice stirs me further as I fight against a heavy blanket of darkness holding me under. When I blink my eyes open, it takes me a minute to rub the sand out and bring the room into focus. Sorcha, Samuel, and Molly are worriedly standing over me. I attempt to sit up in a hurry, but find gravity is not my friend at the moment. Something is also taped to my arm, poking me. Lifting my irritated limb to get a closer look, I see a stupid IV lodged there, feeding me fluids from a bag above.

"Jade, princess, you okay?" Samuel's hand takes mine, wrapping it up in its comfort.

"I'm fine. What the hell happened?" I croak past the thorns caught in my throat.

"The doctor told said you were knocked up, and you passed out, hard. We brought you to the hospital. Turns out, you've been forgetting to eat again, and you needed to be hydrated big time." Sorcha worriedly takes my other hand.

"No fucking hospital. Get me out of here now!" Panic creeps in, flashbacks of the past threatening to set in as I clutch the sheets drawn up around my waist and throw them back.

"Jade, it's gonna be okay. You only need to stay the night." Molly tries to reason with me, trying to pull the covers back over my bare legs.

My hands fly up and grab Samuel by the collar, pulling him into a death hold. "Sam, get me the fuck out of here, now."

He swallows hard before prying my hands off his shirt. "Sor, can't you take care of her at home?"

"Yeah, of course. I'll go have the nurse get the attending for me to talk to." She pats my hand and heads out.

I reach to rip the IV out of my arm, but Samuel stops me. "No way. You are getting that last bag or we are not busting you out of this joint," he cautions.

"Fine." I grimace and pick at my horrid hospital gown.

"Is it safe to say the highlander is the father?" Samuel jests.

"Oh god. That—I didn't make that up in a dream?" I gulp.

"No, honey, you are preggers." Molly tries to put a lid on her happiness over the matter, but it spills through.

"Yes, it's Shae's. Oh Lord, what am I going to do?" I feel as if I am going to pass out again.

"Calm down, you are going to have a baby. We are all going to help you with it and spoil the crap out of it, too," Samuel informs me in his Dom voice.

"No offense, but that doesn't make me feel any better." I sink deeper into the hard bed, my mind spinning out of control.

"Woman, you've really got to get off that hamster wheel in your head." Samuel shoos me over and climbs on the bed, pulling me into his arms.

"So, are you finally going to call him now?" Molly sets my cell phone in my lap as Samuel runs a hand up and down my arm.

"Give me a day. I need to swallow this pill on my own first. If I don't tell him after tomorrow, you have my permission to do it for me."

"Deal." Molly pulls up a chair next to the bed and leans in as we wait for the mighty Sorcha to pull some strings to bust me out of this joint.

Chapter 15

<hr>

Jade

The ocean laps at my feet as I stand alone under the dark sky on the little beach by Sorcha's house. I've been here since yesterday. Thank goodness, they allowed me to come home with my bestie rather than stay another second in that godforsaken place. My hands shake in the aftershock of the vivid memories that came with that experience. I struggle to steady them as I cup the small paper lantern, the warmth radiating from the flickering flame within.

"I love you, Jack, with every fiber of my being. That will never change. Somehow, a few miracles found their way into my broken soul and patched me up. I may be a little sea-worn, but I am good as new. Part of me thinks you had something to do with all of this. It is just like you to find a selfless way to make me happy at all costs. I could stand here and tell you how much I wish it were you, that I wish you were going to be a dad, and we were going to raise a baby together, but I'm not. In a way, your spirit will always be imprinted in this miracle.

"The truth is, Jack, that another has stolen my heart, and it is time to let you go. I can't bear the burden of feeling like I have to hold onto two men at the same time, like there can only be room for one. So, I am letting it all go. I am giving it over to God to hold for me. You will always be tattooed on my heart, Jack, but Shae is, too. You already know he's worth the risk, worth the leap into the tormenting affliction of falling in deep for someone. It's kinda liberating, Jack, to let go and fall into the arms of everything that feels so very right. I couldn't tell him then, and I sure as hell need to get my shit together to find a way to tell him now, but I really am in love with him. He may never speak to me again, but I owe it to him, and the life now growing within me, to try for some sort of reciprocity for all that he gave me and I made a mess of. You know how hardheaded I am, a damn fool, too. Shae gave and gave and all I did was ultimately run from the fear of him trying to replace you. No one can ever replace you.

"When I was sitting in the hospital bed, trying not to lose my mind, I realized something. It never was about replacing you, not at all. Nope, it was about letting go of the pain and agony from your loss to make room for love. You see, Jack, love is limitless… endless… There is never a need to try to confine it to a small space or bind it in any way. By letting go of all the things I thought were supposed to be, and all the suffering I endured by trying to control outcomes, I realized the bountiful abundance waiting for me, and all it can encompass without the stupid limitations we try to place. As humans, we get so caught up in the game of scarcity, locked into this ideal that we must obtain, hoard, and gorge on whatever we desire, as there is a certain end coming to take it away from us. And if it is taken away, we mourn the loss to the point of self-deprecation. That is where we are going wrong. The abundance all around us is fluid, always there to give us more than what we need. It just sometimes has to shift forms or change our story a bit. Losing you was the hardest thing I have ever been through. However, the ample love remains. This means there is room for Shae, too. So, Jack, you sneaky devil, it's time to say our final goodbyes. I will think of you fondly and often, but no longer will it be shadowed with grief. It will only be lit with gratitude for the gift of time and love you gave me. Goodbye, my love." The rising tide sweeps around my ankles as I step further into the tide, soaking the bottom of my long, white skirt.

Bending at the hips, I gently place the lantern in the water. The little beacon of light blinks as the churning ocean waves become bolder with the fast-approaching storm rolling in. I feel marvelous, like a gorilla has jumped off my back. Hitching up the lengths of my hippy skirt, I wade back out the water, the salty spray tainting my lips, swelling the overcoming joy in my heart. I giggle to myself as the clouds above thicken with mist, and then catch a glimpse of a tall figure coming toward me. I let go of my skirt and my jaw drops as I realize who it is. Copper red hair shines out against the greying light, his collar standing against the chill as his well-dressed figure comes at me on a mission. There are no words, no screams of delight as we lock eyes and our feet bring us nearer in a gravitational pull. My heart kicks into overdrive as he fast approaches and reaches forward, the heat of him radiating across my freezing cheek before his skin makes contact. His bright blue eyes sparkle, crinkling slightly in relief as he quickly looks over me before crashing his heavenly lips into mine. Strong arms encapsulate my shivering body as he holds me tighter than I've ever been held before. The embrace is more intimate and raw then being naked and bound before him. I begin to shake in his arms, dumbfounded and unsure that this is really happening. Pulling away from his kiss, I stare up into his eyes.

"Where'd you come from?" I breathe.

"I was about to ask ye the same, my angel." He winks, that damn dimple of his melting my heart.

"Seriously, this can't be real." Maybe I did hit my head at the clinic yesterday.

"It's real. Gavin is pretty damn useful." He winks. Shae really up and left his work to fly all this way, face the overprotective Gavin, and track me down.

"Fuck, Shae, I'm so sorry about everything. I was being stupid. I do love you. I *am* in love with you…" I begin to ramble, but he cuts me off with his searing lips once more, drinking me in with everything he has. This time, the pace is slow and deliberate. He is pouring his entire heart into the kiss, into me. Tears stream down my cheeks as I open to him, completely awestruck and feeling most unworthy.

"Lass, why are ye cryin'?" His fingers chase away the streaks as concern lights him up.

"I feel like a total asshole. I don't deserve you." There, I verbalized my internal fears and insecurities of not feeling worthy of someone like him.

"Hush now, quit talkin' the piss." He laughs and pulls me closer.

"Sir, are you implying that I may be drunk?" I attempt to feign an offensive tone but fail.

"Certainly must be if ye be thinkin' those things. Yer the most valorous person I know. I feel like the ass for not comin' here after ye sooner." Thunder cracks overhead, the humidity thickening around us.

"Being drunk would be an easier explanation, but those days are on hold for another seven months or so—" Based on the shift in the face now warping into a shocked one, I realize my slip of tongue. I hadn't told him about the baby yet. I have been a coward since finding out and couldn't find a way to send a single one of the hundred text messages I had contrived… and deleted.

"Yer pregnant?" He face becomes hard to read, making me insecure all over again.

"Um… yeah."

"I'm the father?"

"Of course you are!" How could he think otherwise? My legs tremble as rain lightly patters on our clothes, seeping into us.

"Well, ye up and left me so fast, and ye told me ye couldn't have kids. I have to ask the question to be sure, Jade." He's right, and the whole thing surprised the hell out of me too. God, I am such a bitch.

"How many times and ways do I need to say I am so very sorry, Shae?" My head hangs in shame. His palm gently lifts it back up, forcing me to meet his gaze.

"Ye mean to tell me we are havin' us a baby?" Excitement lines his handsome features, clueing me into how he is taking all of this.

"Yes."

"That's fuckin' fantastic!" he shouts and picks me up under the arms before swinging me around in a circle. As he slows, my legs instinctively wrap around his waist as I hold on tight. He brings me in closer to claim my mouth as he easily holds my weight now draped around him. The skies above rip open with another earsplitting crack as the heavens rain down, the waves crashing behind us in applause. Joy and love encompass us, kissing the moment of our reunion, sealing our spirits together in a blending unburdened by the past, completely exposed and hopeful for the future. I will embrace it whole-heartedly as it comes and never lose my way again.

Epilogue

Jade

"God, I can't do this anymore." Sorcha moans from the couch where she's been beached with her big belly.

"Any day now, Momma." I snort a laugh. She's had a miserable pregnancy. Thankfully, mine has been pretty amazing. I've loved every minute and haven't had any issues.

"Just you wait; this is going to be you soon." Her hand sweeps over her belly before tenderly embracing it. She bitches a lot, but she loves it at the same time.

The ocean breeze floats in through the open window in her living room, bringing the call of the seagulls with it. My heart aches, missing my man. Shae's been working back and forth between here and Glasgow. Moving his office to San Francisco permanently has been harder than we anticipated. He finally gets back tomorrow.

"You look lost in thought... missing a tall, dark, and ginger?" She huffs and puffs as she tries to get her glass of water off the table.

"Yeah, tomorrow, I finally get to fall asleep while having someone rub my shoulders."

"You two think any further on setting a date?"

Shae had purposed a few months ago back in Scotland when we visited his family together. I love them, his grandad especially. The whole thing was sweet. He drove me up to his grandad's house, set up a picnic on the beach, and popped the question. It was ridiculously cold and windy. We soon packed it into the cottage and finished by the fire, but it was memorable all the same.

"Nah, maybe summer next year. I'm in no hurry. Cart is already before the horse." As if on cue, the bundle in my belly starts kicking. I will never get used to a human kicking me this hard from the inside, but it's so freaking cool.

"You gonna do it over there or here?"

"I want to have everyone go over there and do it." Shae's grandad can't travel like he used to, and, honestly, it felt more special to do it there rather than here, something authentic to us… rather than reliving another San Francisco wedding.

I smile to myself as my hand rubs my belly; our son begins to play soccer as his little feet bang against my hand. We wanted to wait to find out, but when we went in for the ultrasound and they asked if we wanted to know, I blurted out a yes. Shae laughed at me, said he knew my inquisitive nature would get the best of me. My phone beeps an incoming message, and I shift to grab the phone off the end table.

How are my angels doing? I'm boarding now. Will be there to wrap the two of you in my arms by morning.

I smile, and my heart skips a beat, more than ready to have him back. With each day, I come to love him more and more, if that's even possible.

He's kicking me senseless, ready for your soothing voice to calm him down. Safe travels. I can't wait to kiss you.

"Fuck! Oh, shit," Sorcha screams, causing me to drop my phone and waddle out of the chair.

"What? Is it time?" I ask as I hover over her, looking her over as she clutches her belly.

"Yes! Oh, fuck me. Call Gavin to get us." She moans before taking a deep breath, the contraction slowly easing its grip on her.

I palm my phone and do as I am told, grabbing her slip-on shoes by the door and sliding them on her feet as the phone rings and rings. "Sor, he isn't answering." I hang up as soon as the voice mail picks up and hit redial.

"That fucker better not be off on some secret spy shit for Daz or they both are getting castrated. He's not missing the delivery of his daughter!" She grunts, beginning to shift and shimmy her fat ass, trying to get up from the couch.

"What are you doing? Sit down; I will get the bag and everything. You need to sit down before you break something," I scold.

"Woman, this baby isn't coming for a while. First-time deliveries usually take forever. If my contractions start coming hard and fast, we will hurry it—fuck!" She curses and begins breathing through the next contraction. I give up dialing Gavin, hang up, and send him a text to get his ass to the midwives.

"Yeah, and I bet she makes her own hard-and-fast rules just like her momma. As soon as that one is done, waddle your stubborn ass to the car. I'll grab the bag."

It doesn't take long before I have her loaded up, screaming all sorts of obscenities as I book it to the birthing center. Thankfully, they picked up on the first attempt, and I was able to alert them to the mess that about to descend upon them. Sorcha wanted to do a home birth, and Gavin wanted her to be in the hospital, so the midwives were the best compromise.

Twenty minutes later, we pull up. The staff is waiting at the entrance with a wheelchair, battle faces in place.

"Oh God, Jade, I need to push!"

"Listen here—you are not birthing that kid in my car. Get your ass into that wheelchair." I throw the car into park, rush out, and open her door.

She looks up at me with uncertainty, her sweat-soaked hair matted about her porcelain face and hands trembling around her belly.

"Sor, you got this. I'm not leaving your side. You are not alone." I hold my hand out to her as the staff positions the chair to my side so that she can stand, pivot, and immediately sit into it.

"Okay, we got this." She hauls herself up, forgoing my hand, and barely makes it into the waiting chair before another one hits.

"How many minutes apart are the contractions?" a nurse asks over her shoulder as they usher her inside.

"Like three to four minutes, and she's having pressure!" I yell as I quickly make to park the car and head in after them.

I make it inside the sliding doors, hearing Sorcha all the way down the hall cursing in Gaelic, truly in a mad state. I check my phone for any response from Gavin as I hurry toward her.

"Miss? You are?" A nurse stops me in the hall.

"I'm her best friend and the only one who might have a chance in hell to get her to cooperate with you until her husband gets here."

A loud crash and thud sounds out, followed by a screamed, "Where the fuck is Gavin!"

"Right this way." She gives me a look and leads the way. Not that I need help finding her.

Pushing open the door to her suite, I quickly duck as something metal goes flying past my head. It hits the wall and clatters to the ground by my feet. It is a speculum of some sort. My brow hits the ceiling, not sure how she got her hands on that.

I glance up from the device to see her white knuckling the bedrails as she begins to breathe hard, sending everyone in the room a death glare. I struggle not to laugh. But the harder I try not to, the more it tries to come.

"Fuck you, Jade. Where is he?" she snarls in a demonic tone. I bust up, right there, on the spot, at the seams. The staff and their mortified glances keep shifting back and forth between us like we are completely bonkers.

"He's parking." I hold up the phone with his message and bring it forward so she can see. She grasps for it, but I yank it away, knowing full well she will chuck it too. She growls at my quick reflexes. Another contraction begins to wrap around her abdomen. She starts to huff like a puffer fish, grabs the pillows behind her, and throws them across the room, smack into the plastic blinds.

"Sorcha, calm down," Gavin's voice commands in a boom from behind me, and I sneak a silent thanks up to God as I step aside. His large build comes to loom over the bed as he takes her hand in his, pressing his forehead to hers. The contact shifts her instantly into a calm, collected mother-to-be, valiantly breathing through the pain without so much as a knife flying through the air.

After this one passes, Gavin turns to the hesitant nurse in the corner who has monitoring equipment in her hands intended for Sorcha. "Come on then." He waves her over. She quickly sets up everything, and the baby's heartbeat blares to life in the room as the monitor comes on.

"I'd like to examine you now to see how much you've dilated," the nurse informs Sor.

"Fuck no. I need to push. I've needed to push since the damn car ride over!" She howls as the next force battles through her womb.

Gavin assumes the previous position, her hand death gripping his as they breathe together through it. His rhythmic voice begins to soothe her, and then informs her she's going to let the nurse examine her. With a few more curses, Sorcha agrees, and they make quick work of it.

"Oh yeah, it is time. I will go get the midwife!" The nurse runs off.

"I told you all it was time!" Sorcha groans and her head falls back, exhaustion getting the best of her. She doesn't get to rest long before another fit takes over.

Within no time at all, the staff is all surrounding her, I am on one side of the bed, Gavin on the other as she attempts to break our hands while birthing a new life into the world. When little Abigail Rose makes her entrance and is placed on her mother's bare chest, tears are streaming down our faces as we lovingly crowd around Mom and baby. It is one of the most beautiful moments I have ever been blessed to be a part of. It all makes me so very happy, and quite ecstatic for Shae to return.

But what does me in good is the sight of Abigail all bundled up, being cradled by her giant father as he tenderly rocks her and coos sweet sounds. That's when the silent tears and yearning for my man really starts up. That's going to be us in just a few short months, and I can't wait.

The End…for now ;)
Stay Tuned for the next installment of the Affliction of Falling Series where we get to know more about the mysterious man in Molly's life, and, not to worry, you will continue to get updates and insights on the whole crew.
Follow the author, Kristina Canady @
www.KristinaCanady.com
Facebook: www.facebook.com/midnightbloompart1
Twitter:
@KristinaCanady

Made in the USA
Lexington, KY
30 April 2017